Pokémon™

BLACK AND WHITE

VOL.17

Story by **HIDENORI KUSAKA**
Art by **SATOSHI YAMAMOTO**

BLACK AND WHITE

Pokémon Black and White
Volume 17
Perfect Square Edition

Story by HIDENORI KUSAKA
Art by SATOSHI YAMAMOTO

© 2014 Pokémon.
© 1995–2014 Nintendo/Creatures Inc./GAME FREAK inc.
TM, ®, and character names are trademarks of Nintendo.
POCKET MONSTERS SPECIAL (Magazine Edition)
by Hidenori KUSAKA, Satoshi YAMAMOTO
© 1997 Hidenori KUSAKA, Satoshi YAMAMOTO
All rights reserved.
Original Japanese edition published by SHOGAKUKAN.
English translation rights in the United States of America, Canada, the United Kingdom,
Ireland, Australia and New Zealand arranged with SHOGAKUKAN.

English Adaptation / Bryant Turnage
Translation / Tetsuichiro Miyaki
Touch-up & Lettering / Susan Daigle-Leach
Cover Art Assistance / Miguel Riebman
Design / Fawn Lau
Editor / Annette Roman

Printed in the U.S.A.

Published by VIZ Media, LLC
P.O. Box 77010
San Francisco, CA 94107

10 9 8 7 6 5 4 3 2 1
First printing, August 2014

www.perfectsquare.com

www.viz.com

PARENTAL ADVISORY
POKÉMON ADVENTURES
is rated A and is suitable
for readers of all ages.
ratings.viz.com

POKÉMON™

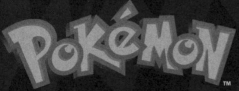

BLACK AND WHITE

VOL. 17

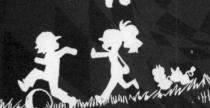

THE STORY THUS FAR!

Pokémon Trainer Black is exploring the mysterious Unova region with his brand-new Pokédex. Pokémon Trainer White runs a thriving talent agency for performing Pokémon. While traveling together, their paths cross with Team Plasma, a nefarious group that advocates releasing your Pokémon into the wild! Now Black and White are off on their own separate journeys of discovery...

BLACK'S dream is to win the Pokémon League!

WHITE'S dream is to work in show biz... and now she's learning how to Pokémon Battle as well!

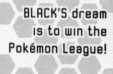

Black's Munna, MUSHA, helps him think clearly, but now Musha has left him!

White's Tepig, GIGI, and Black's Emboar, BO, get along like peanut butter and jelly! But Gigi left White for another Trainer...

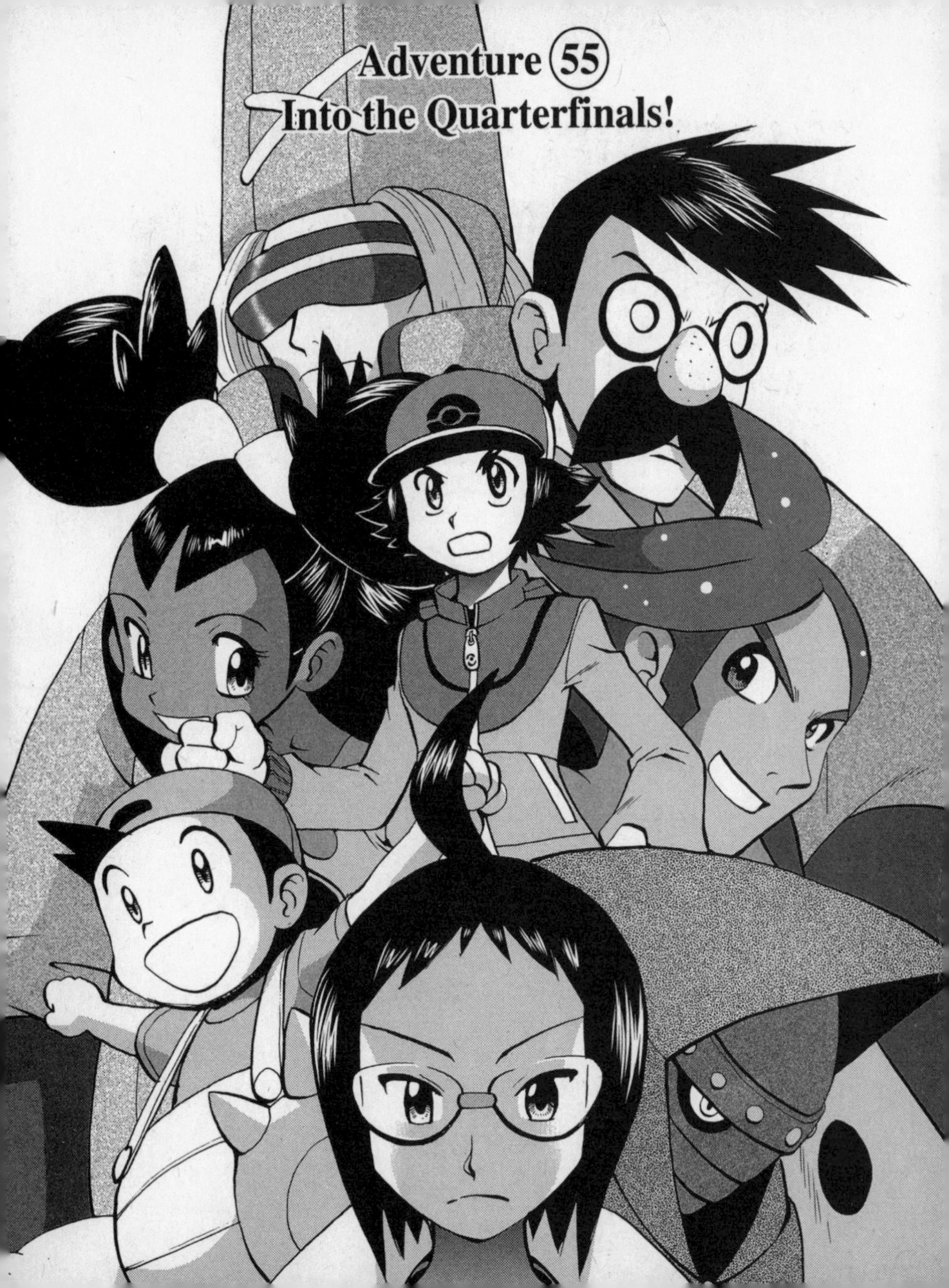
Adventure 55
Into the Quarterfinals!

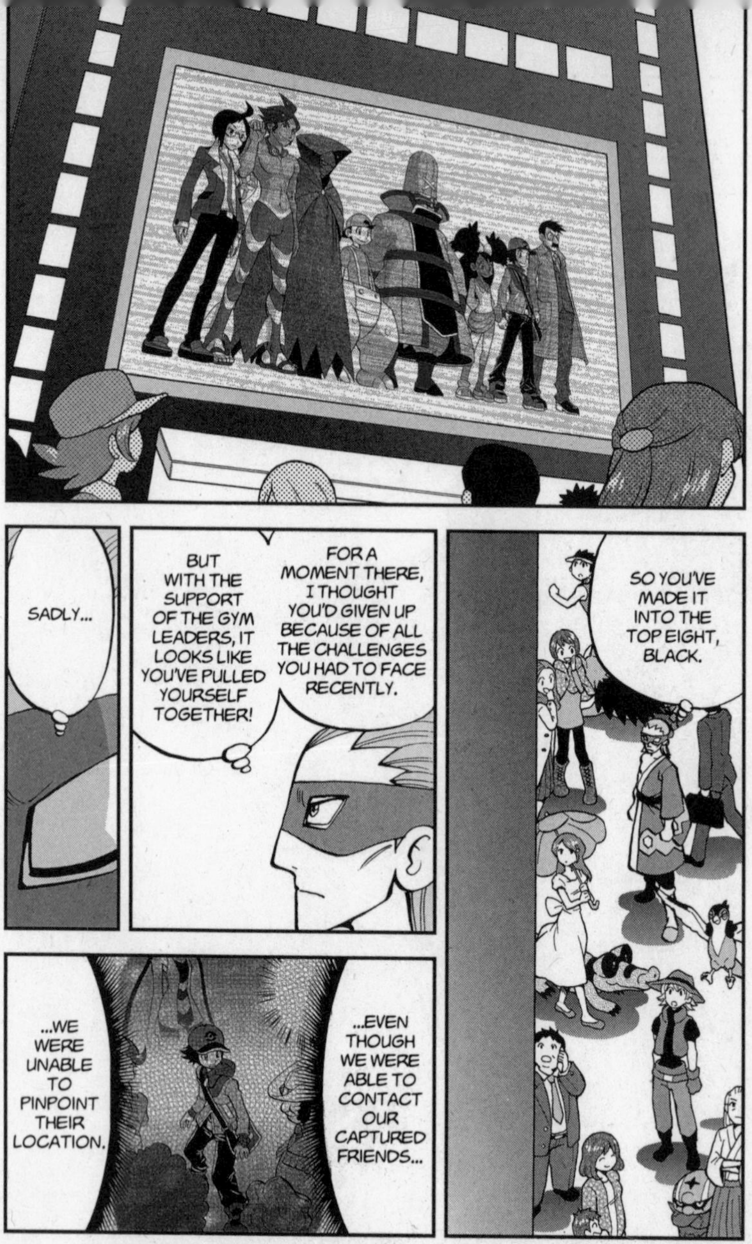
SO YOU'VE MADE IT INTO THE TOP EIGHT, BLACK.
FOR A MOMENT THERE, I THOUGHT YOU'D GIVEN UP BECAUSE OF ALL THE CHALLENGES YOU HAD TO FACE RECENTLY.
BUT WITH THE SUPPORT OF THE GYM LEADERS, IT LOOKS LIKE YOU'VE PULLED YOURSELF TOGETHER!
SADLY...
...EVEN THOUGH WE WERE ABLE TO CONTACT OUR CAPTURED FRIENDS...
...WE WERE UNABLE TO PINPOINT THEIR LOCATION.

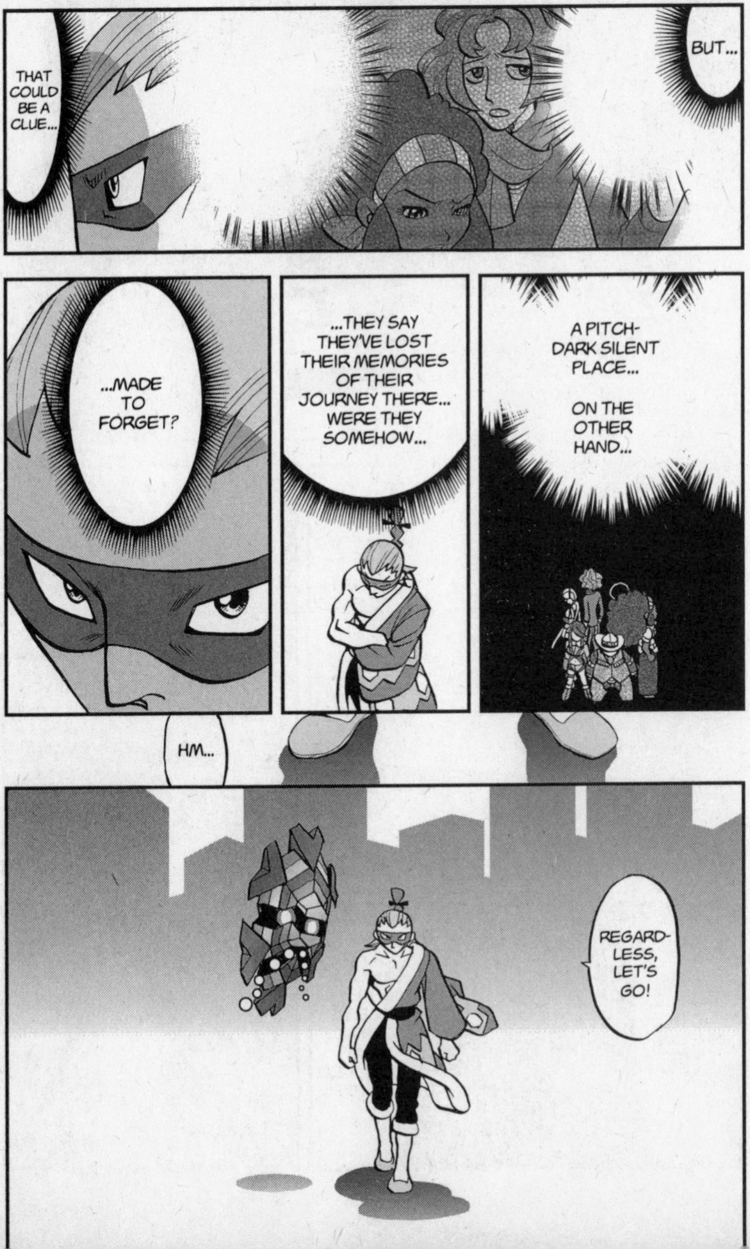
BUT...
THAT COULD BE A CLUE...
A PITCH-DARK SILENT PLACE... ON THE OTHER HAND...
...THEY SAY THEY'VE LOST THEIR MEMORIES OF THEIR JOURNEY THERE... WERE THEY SOMEHOW...
...MADE TO FORGET?
HM...
REGARD-LESS, LET'S GO!

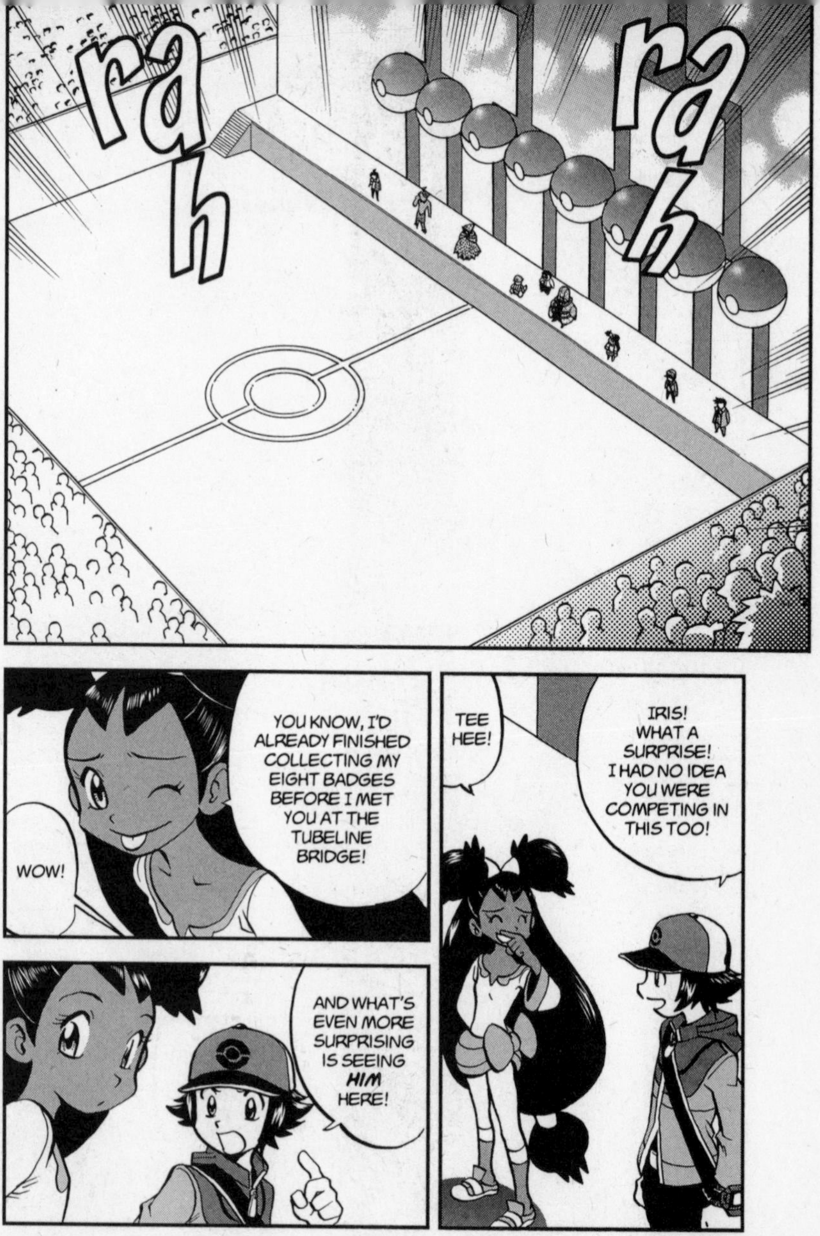

rah
rah
IRIS! WHAT A SURPRISE! I HAD NO IDEA YOU WERE COMPETING IN THIS TOO!
TEE HEE!
YOU KNOW, I'D ALREADY FINISHED COLLECTING MY EIGHT BADGES BEFORE I MET YOU AT THE TUBELINE BRIDGE!
WOW!
AND WHAT'S EVEN MORE SURPRISING IS SEEING **HIM** HERE!

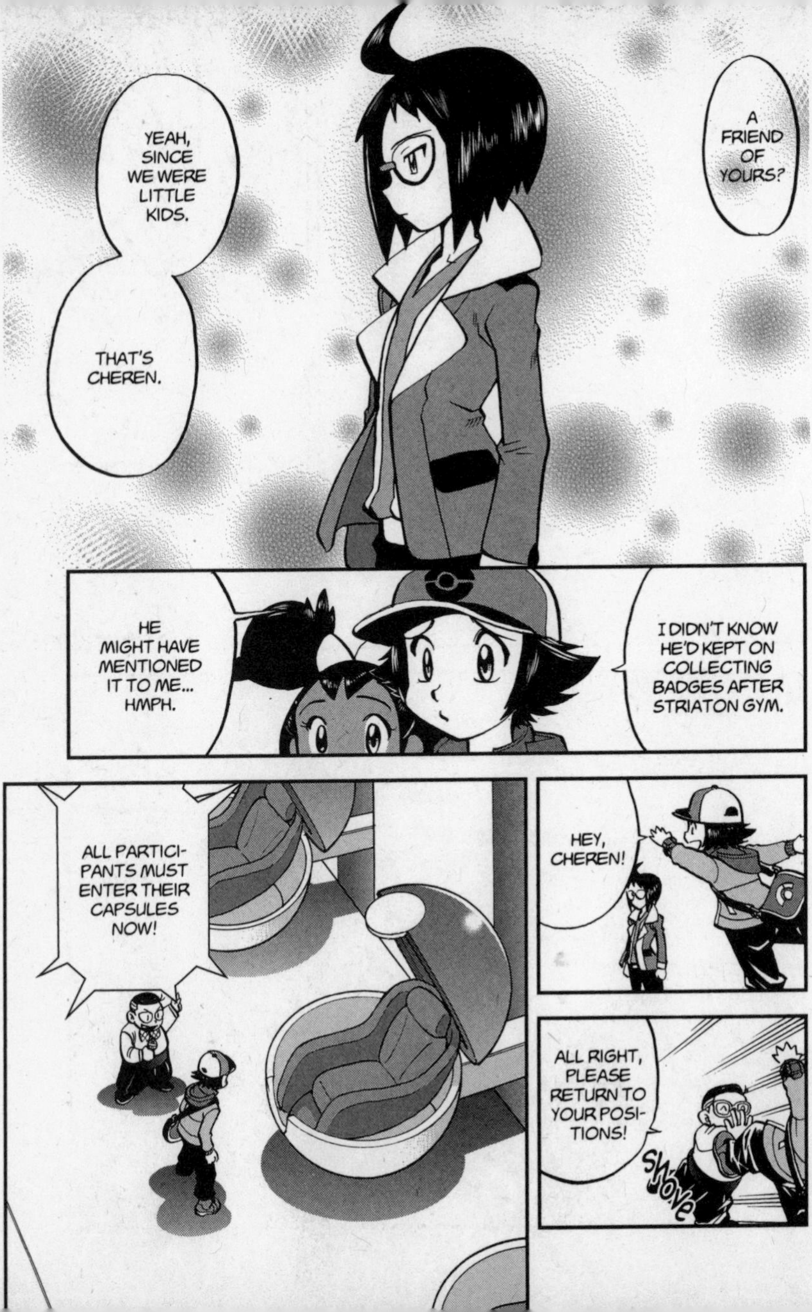
A FRIEND OF YOURS?
YEAH, SINCE WE WERE LITTLE KIDS.
THAT'S CHEREN.
I DIDN'T KNOW HE'D KEPT ON COLLECTING BADGES AFTER STRIATON GYM.
HE MIGHT HAVE MENTIONED IT TO ME... HMPH.
HEY, CHEREN!
ALL RIGHT, PLEASE RETURN TO YOUR POSI-TIONS!
SHOVE
ALL PARTICI-PANTS MUST ENTER THEIR CAPSULES NOW!

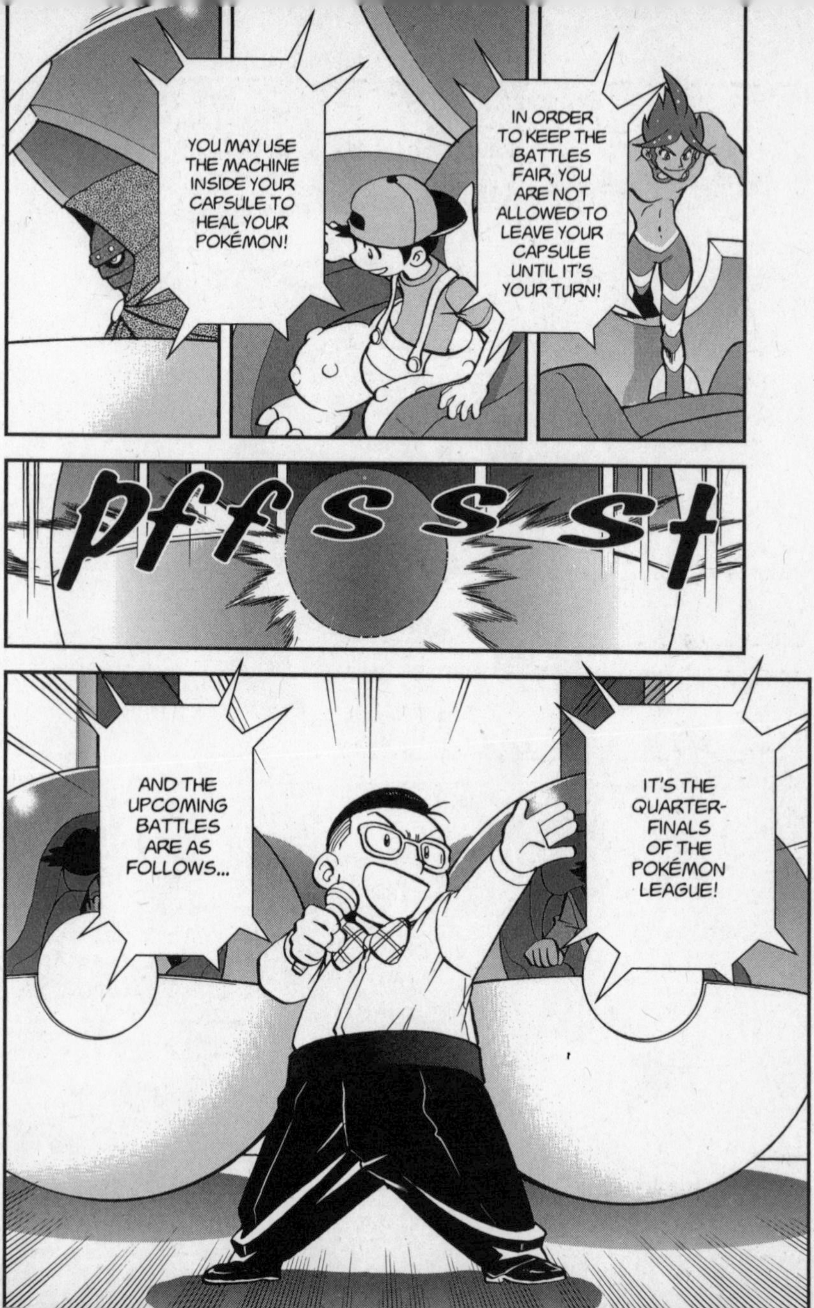
IN ORDER TO KEEP THE BATTLES FAIR, YOU ARE NOT ALLOWED TO LEAVE YOUR CAPSULE UNTIL IT'S YOUR TURN!
YOU MAY USE THE MACHINE INSIDE YOUR CAPSULE TO HEAL YOUR POKÉMON!
pfsssst
IT'S THE QUARTER-FINALS OF THE POKÉMON LEAGUE!
AND THE UPCOMING BATTLES ARE AS FOLLOWS...

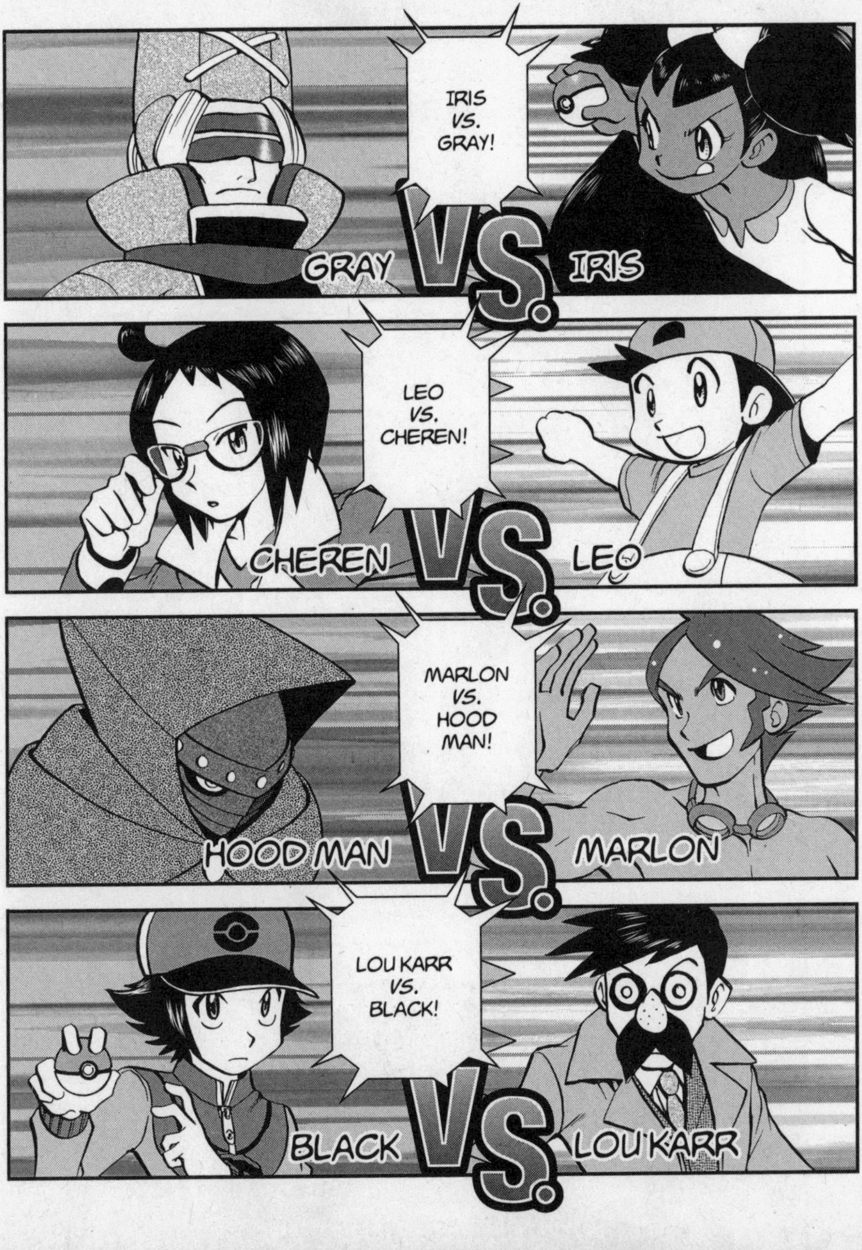
IRIS VS. GRAY!
IRIS
VS.
GRAY
LEO VS. CHEREN!
LEO
VS.
CHEREN
MARLON VS. HOOD MAN!
MARLON
VS.
HOOD MAN
LOU KARR VS. BLACK!
LOU KARR
VS.
BLACK

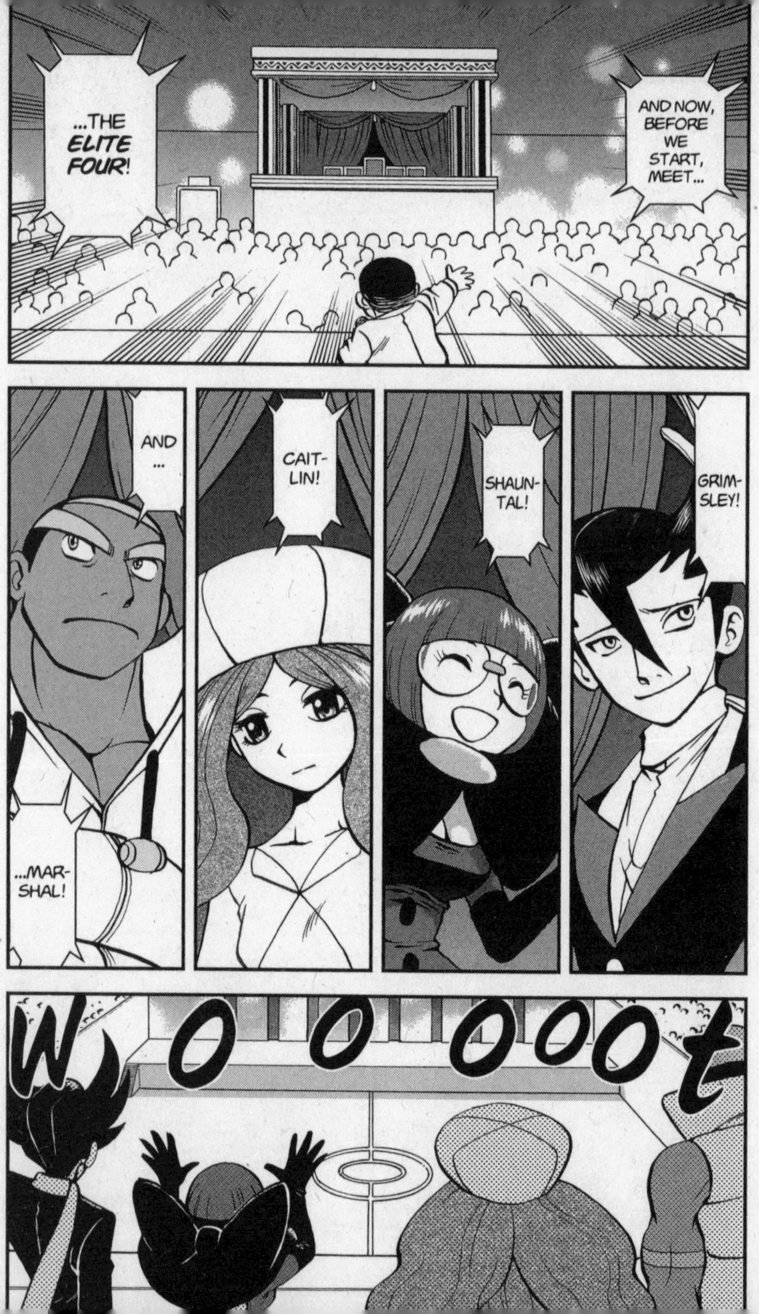
AND NOW, BEFORE WE START, MEET...
...THE *ELITE FOUR*!
GRIM-SLEY!
SHAUN-TAL!
CAIT-LIN!
AND ...
...MAR-SHAL!
WOOOOOt

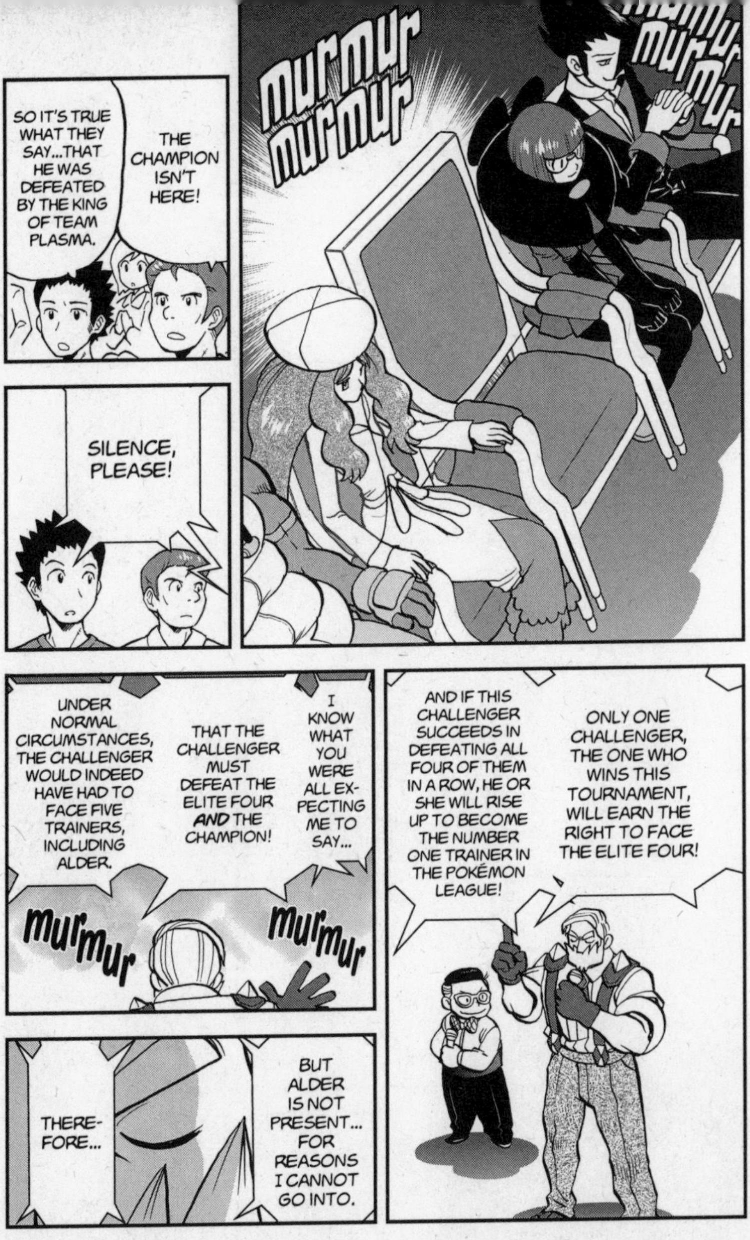
murmur murmur
murmur murmur
THE CHAMPION ISN'T HERE!
SO IT'S TRUE WHAT THEY SAY...THAT HE WAS DEFEATED BY THE KING OF TEAM PLASMA.
SILENCE, PLEASE!
ONLY ONE CHALLENGER, THE ONE WHO WINS THIS TOURNAMENT, WILL EARN THE RIGHT TO FACE THE ELITE FOUR!
AND IF THIS CHALLENGER SUCCEEDS IN DEFEATING ALL FOUR OF THEM IN A ROW, HE OR SHE WILL RISE UP TO BECOME THE NUMBER ONE TRAINER IN THE POKÉMON LEAGUE!
I KNOW WHAT YOU WERE ALL EX-PECTING ME TO SAY...
THAT THE CHALLENGER MUST DEFEAT THE ELITE FOUR AND THE CHAMPION!
UNDER NORMAL CIRCUMSTANCES, THE CHALLENGER WOULD INDEED HAVE HAD TO FACE FIVE TRAINERS, INCLUDING ALDER.
murmur
murmur
BUT ALDER IS NOT PRESENT... FOR REASONS I CANNOT GO INTO.
THERE-FORE...

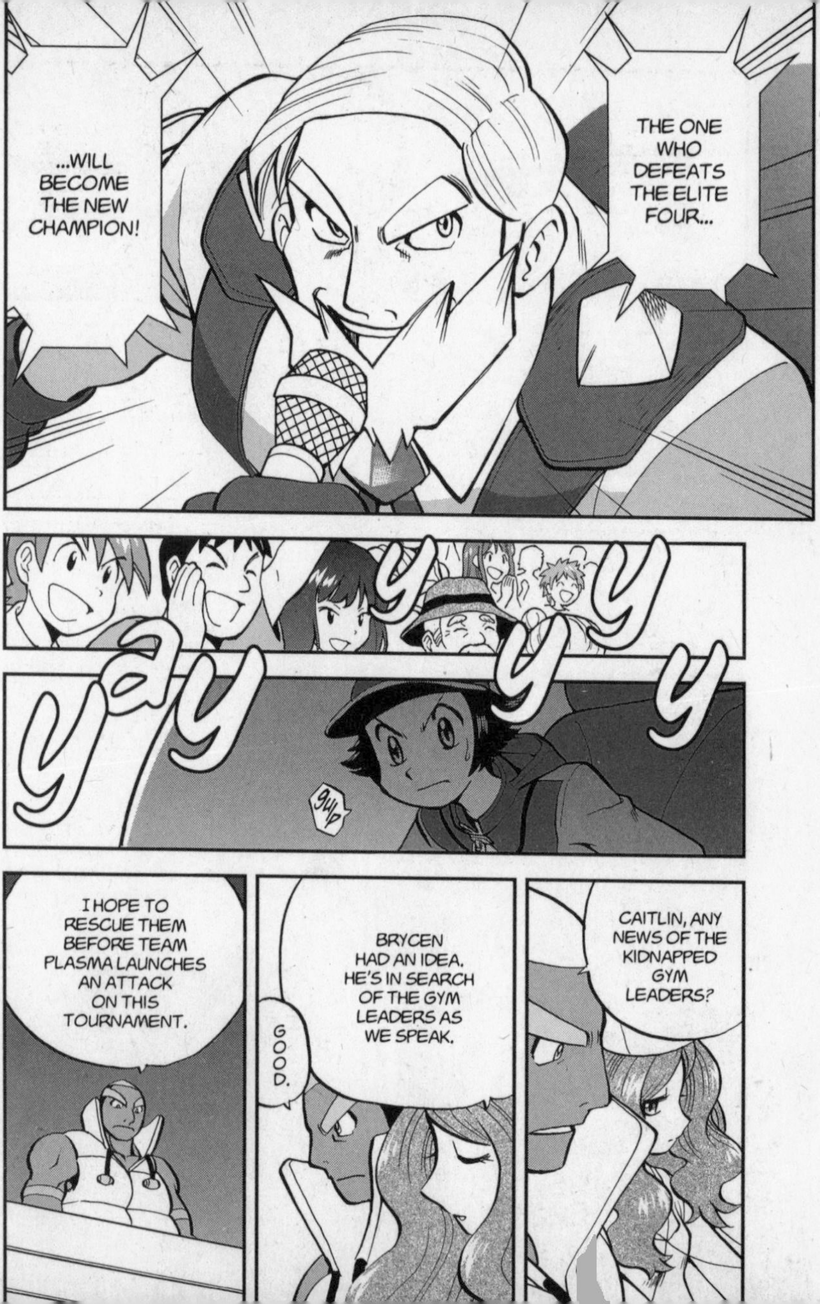
THE ONE WHO DEFEATS THE ELITE FOUR...
...WILL BECOME THE NEW CHAMPION!
yayyyyy
gulp
CAITLIN, ANY NEWS OF THE KIDNAPPED GYM LEADERS?
BRYCEN HAD AN IDEA. HE'S IN SEARCH OF THE GYM LEADERS AS WE SPEAK.
GOOD.
I HOPE TO RESCUE THEM BEFORE TEAM PLASMA LAUNCHES AN ATTACK ON THIS TOURNAMENT.

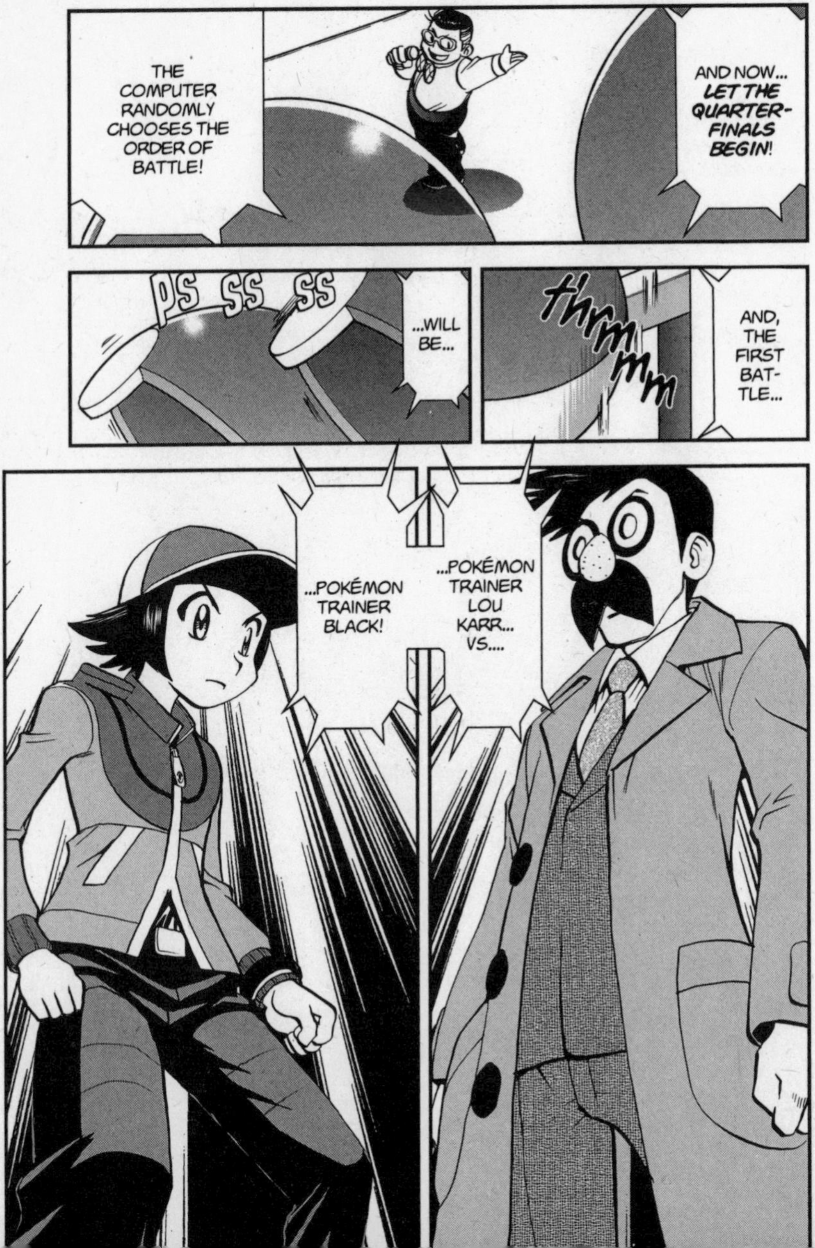
AND NOW... LET THE QUARTER-FINALS BEGIN!
THE COMPUTER RANDOMLY CHOOSES THE ORDER OF BATTLE!
AND, THE FIRST BAT-TLE...
thrmmmm
...WILL BE...
pssss
...POKÉMON TRAINER LOU KARR... VS....
...POKÉMON TRAINER BLACK!

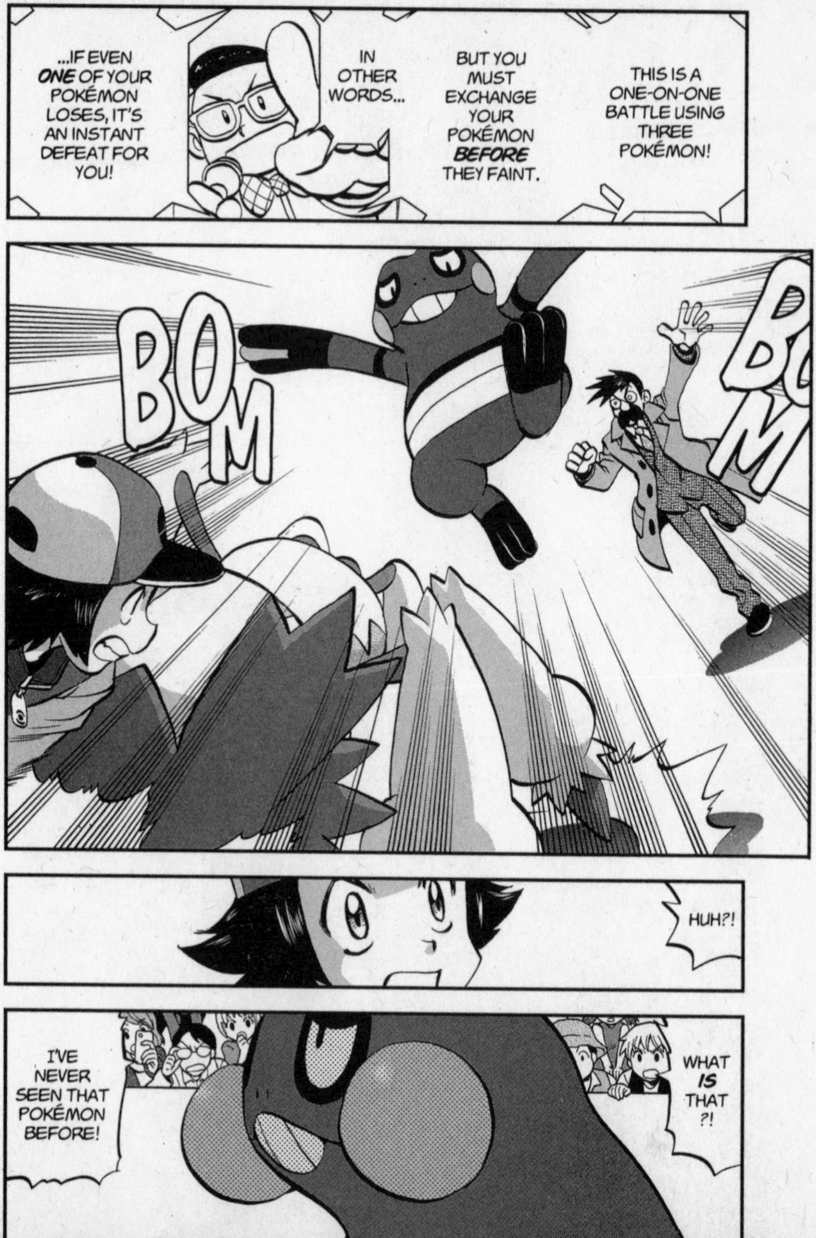
THIS IS A ONE-ON-ONE BATTLE USING THREE POKÉMON!
BUT YOU MUST EXCHANGE YOUR POKÉMON **BEFORE** THEY FAINT.
IN OTHER WORDS...
...IF EVEN **ONE** OF YOUR POKÉMON LOSES, IT'S AN INSTANT DEFEAT FOR YOU!
BOM
BOM
HUH?!
WHAT **IS** THAT?!
I'VE NEVER SEEN THAT POKÉMON BEFORE!

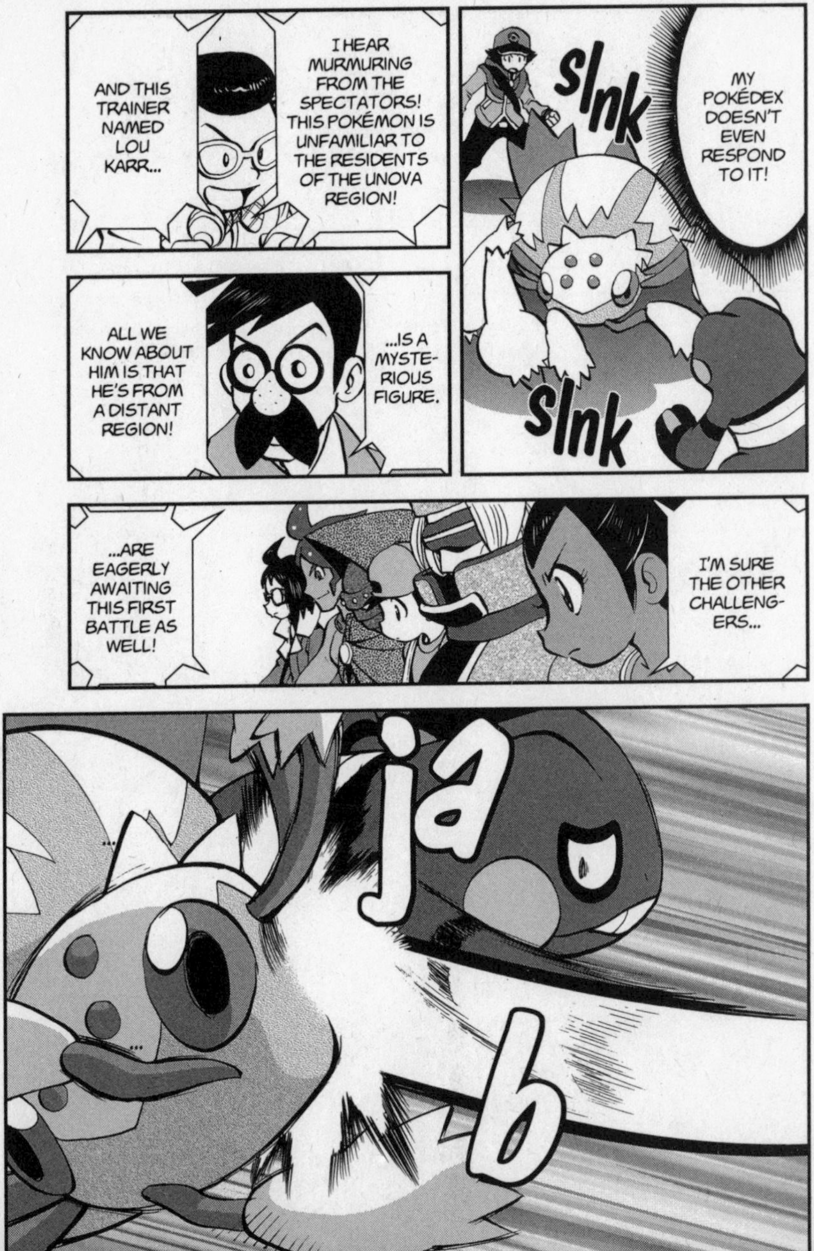
slnk
MY POKÉDEX DOESN'T EVEN RESPOND TO IT!
slnk
I HEAR MURMURING FROM THE SPECTATORS! THIS POKÉMON IS UNFAMILIAR TO THE RESIDENTS OF THE UNOVA REGION!
AND THIS TRAINER NAMED LOU KARR...
...IS A MYSTE-RIOUS FIGURE.
ALL WE KNOW ABOUT HIM IS THAT HE'S FROM A DISTANT REGION!
I'M SURE THE OTHER CHALLENG-ERS...
...ARE EAGERLY AWAITING THIS FIRST BATTLE AS WELL!
jab
...
...

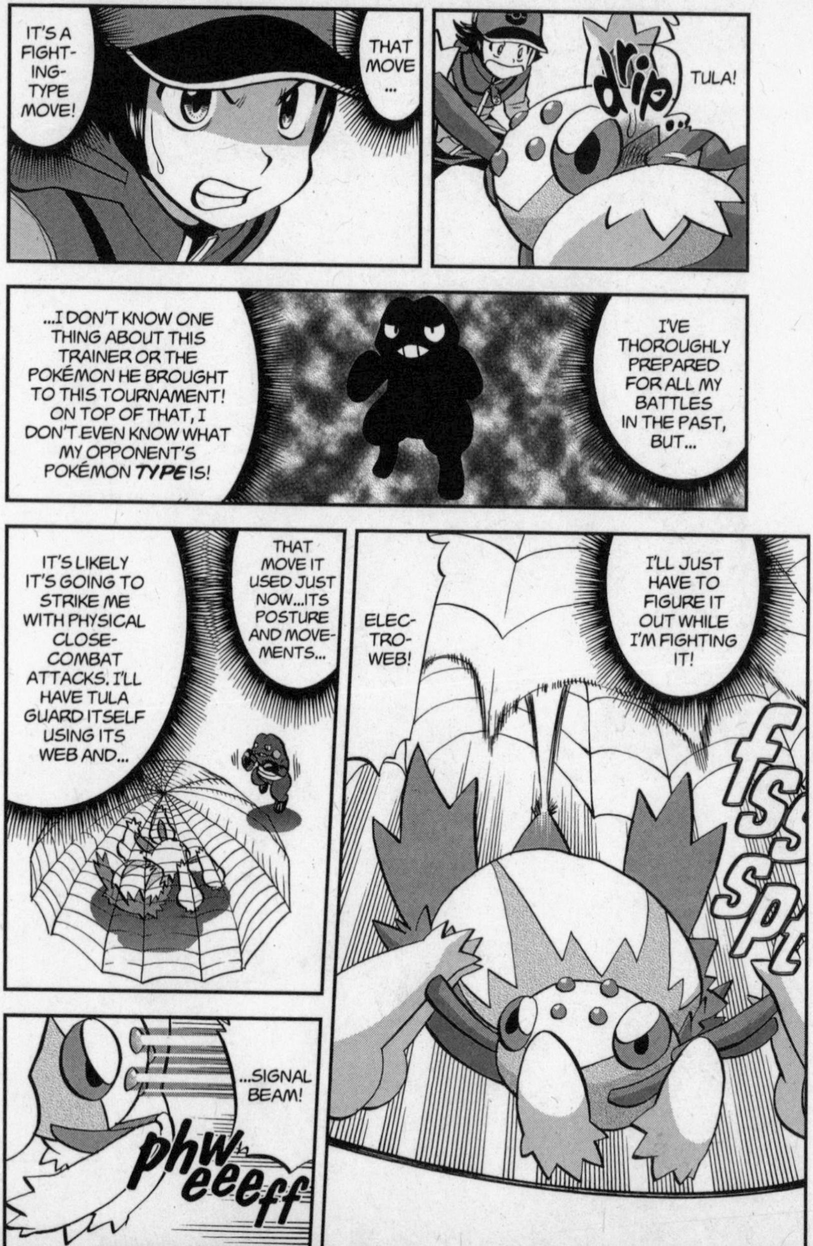

drip...
TULA!
THAT MOVE...
IT'S A FIGHTING-TYPE MOVE!
I'VE THOROUGHLY PREPARED FOR ALL MY BATTLES IN THE PAST, BUT...
...I DON'T KNOW ONE THING ABOUT THIS TRAINER OR THE POKÉMON HE BROUGHT TO THIS TOURNAMENT! ON TOP OF THAT, I DON'T EVEN KNOW WHAT MY OPPONENT'S POKÉMON *TYPE* IS!
I'LL JUST HAVE TO FIGURE IT OUT WHILE I'M FIGHTING IT!
ELECTRO-WEB!
fssspt
THAT MOVE IT USED JUST NOW...ITS POSTURE AND MOVEMENTS...
IT'S LIKELY IT'S GOING TO STRIKE ME WITH PHYSICAL CLOSE-COMBAT ATTACKS. I'LL HAVE TULA GUARD ITSELF USING ITS WEB AND...
...SIGNAL BEAM!
phweeeff

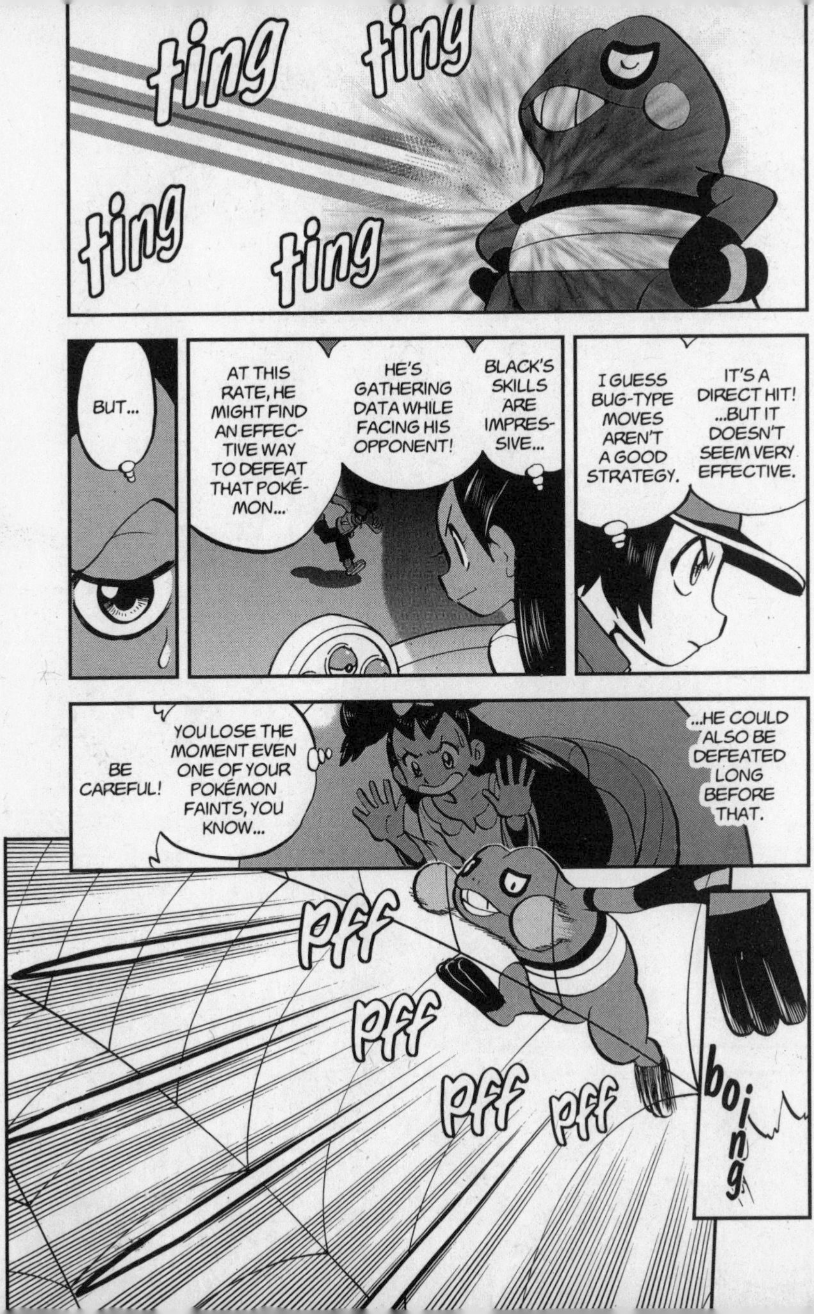
ting
ting
ting
ting
IT'S A DIRECT HIT! ...BUT IT DOESN'T SEEM VERY EFFECTIVE.
I GUESS BUG-TYPE MOVES AREN'T A GOOD STRATEGY.
BLACK'S SKILLS ARE IMPRES-SIVE...
HE'S GATHERING DATA WHILE FACING HIS OPPONENT!
AT THIS RATE, HE MIGHT FIND AN EFFEC-TIVE WAY TO DEFEAT THAT POKÉ-MON...
BUT...
...HE COULD ALSO BE DEFEATED LONG BEFORE THAT.
YOU LOSE THE MOMENT EVEN ONE OF YOUR POKÉMON FAINTS, YOU KNOW...
BE CAREFUL!
boing
pff
pff
pff
pff

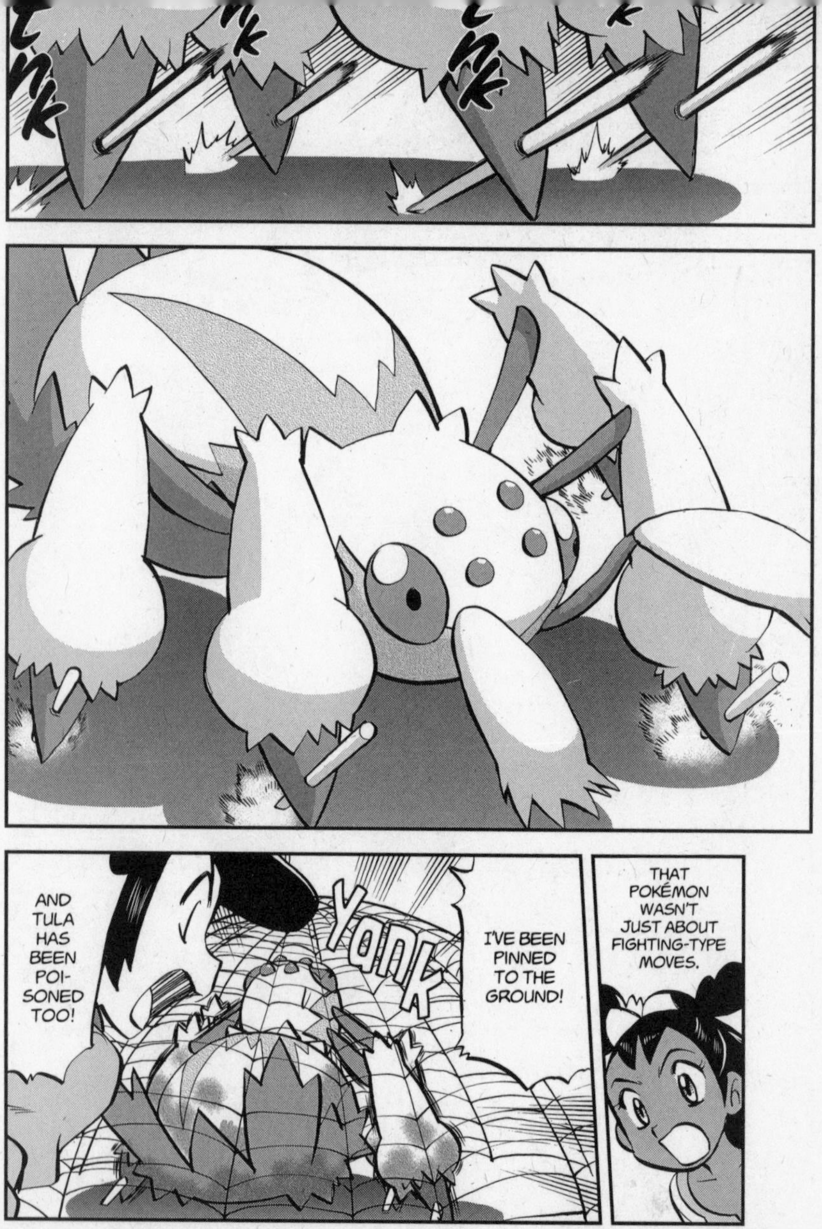
THAT POKÉMON WASN'T JUST ABOUT FIGHTING-TYPE MOVES.
I'VE BEEN PINNED TO THE GROUND!
Yank
AND TULA HAS BEEN POI-SONED TOO!

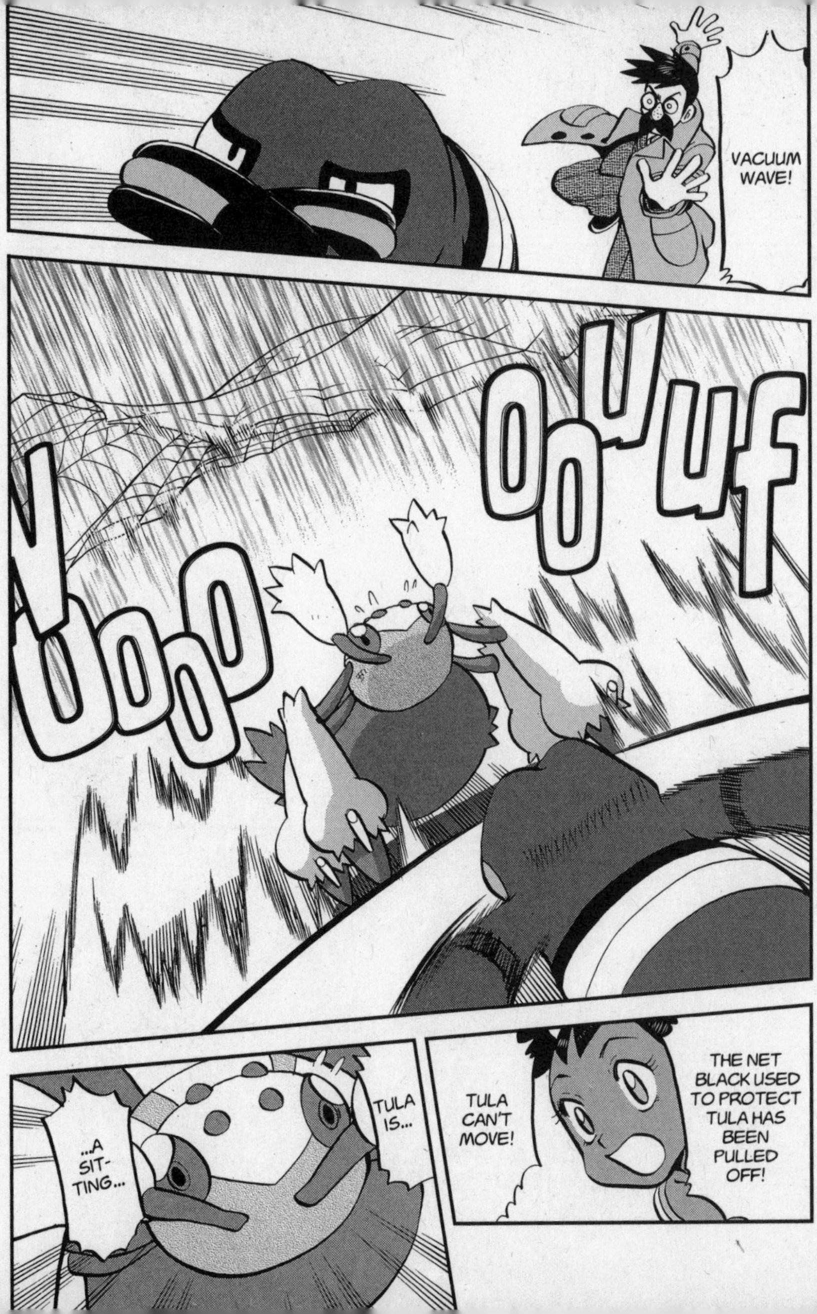
VACUUM WAVE!
OOUUF
OOOO
THE NET BLACK USED TO PROTECT TULA HAS BEEN PULLED OFF!
TULA CAN'T MOVE!
TULA IS...
...A SIT-TING...

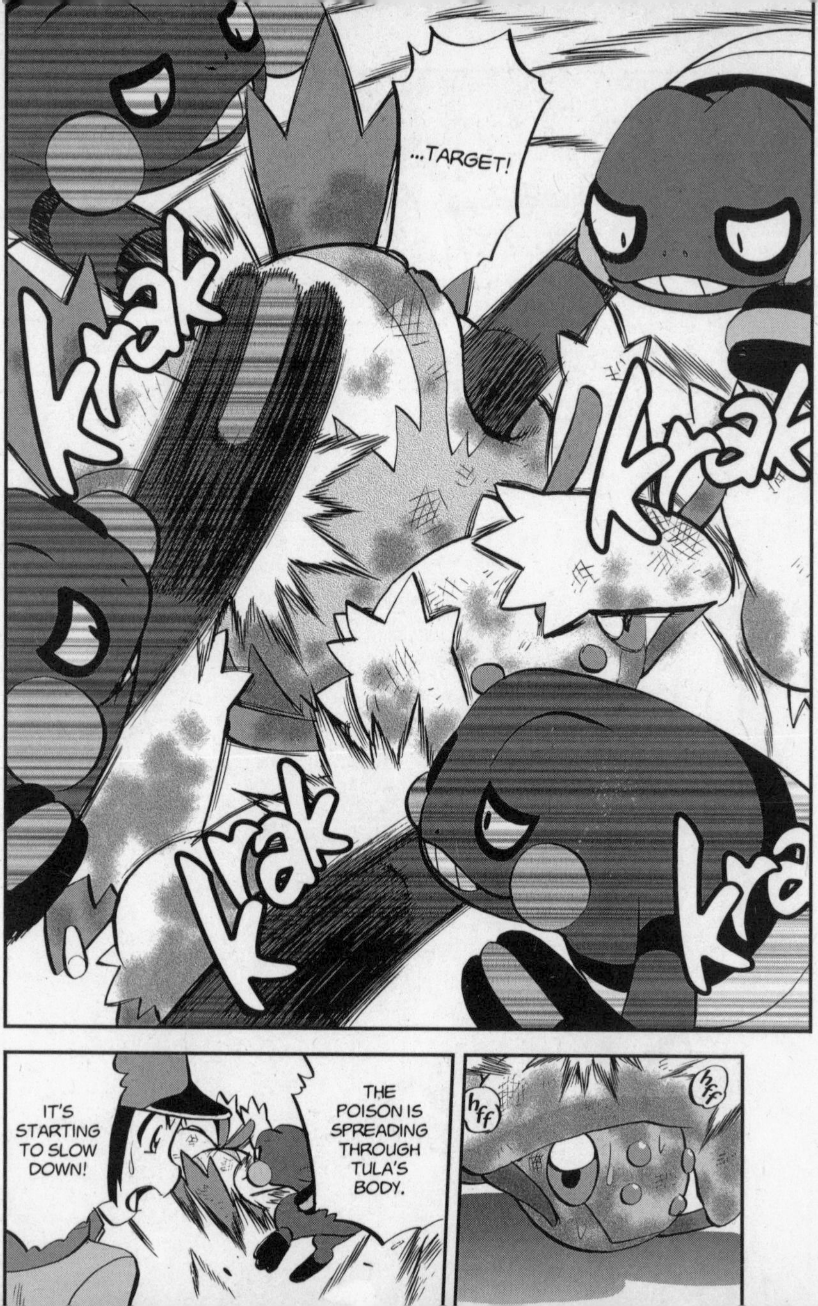
...TARGET!
krak
krak
krak
kra
hff
hff
THE POISON IS SPREADING THROUGH TULA'S BODY.
IT'S STARTING TO SLOW DOWN!

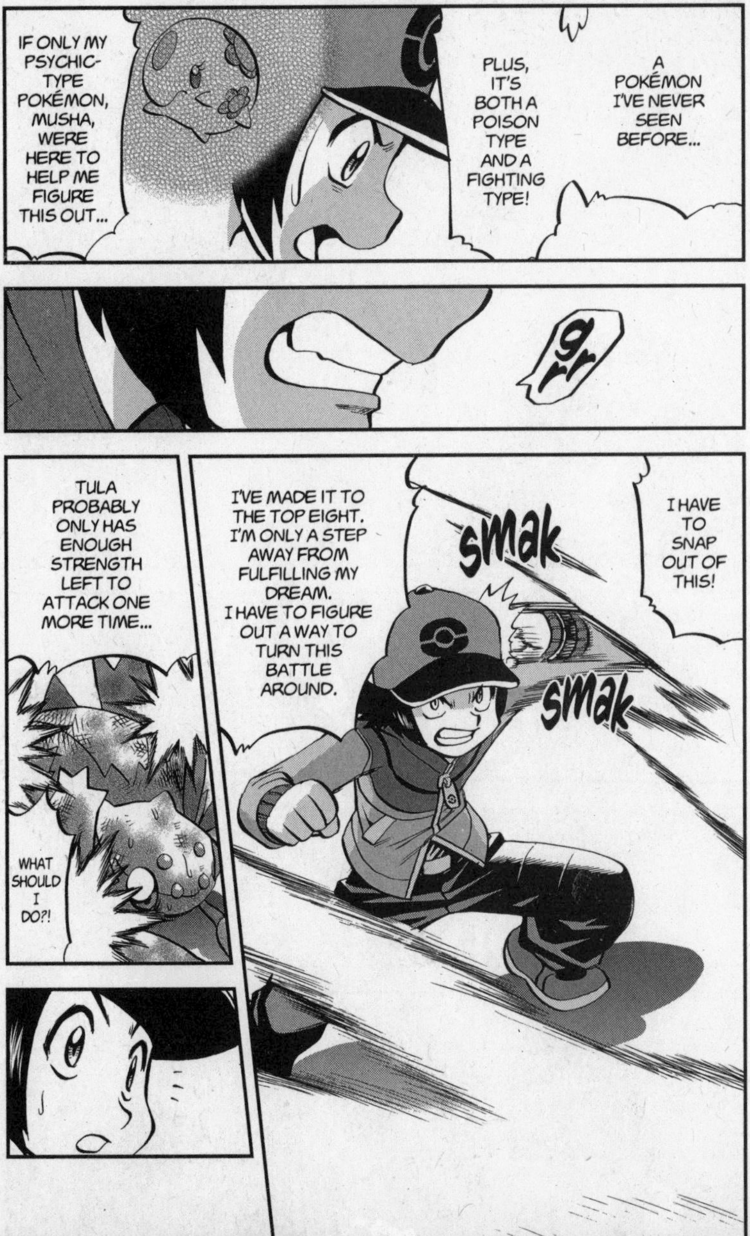
A POKÉMON I'VE NEVER SEEN BEFORE...
PLUS, IT'S BOTH A POISON TYPE AND A FIGHTING TYPE!
IF ONLY MY PSYCHIC-TYPE POKÉMON, MUSHA, WERE HERE TO HELP ME FIGURE THIS OUT...
grr
I HAVE TO SNAP OUT OF THIS!
smak
I'VE MADE IT TO THE TOP EIGHT. I'M ONLY A STEP AWAY FROM FULFILLING MY DREAM. I HAVE TO FIGURE OUT A WAY TO TURN THIS BATTLE AROUND.
smak
TULA PROBABLY ONLY HAS ENOUGH STRENGTH LEFT TO ATTACK ONE MORE TIME...
WHAT SHOULD I DO?!

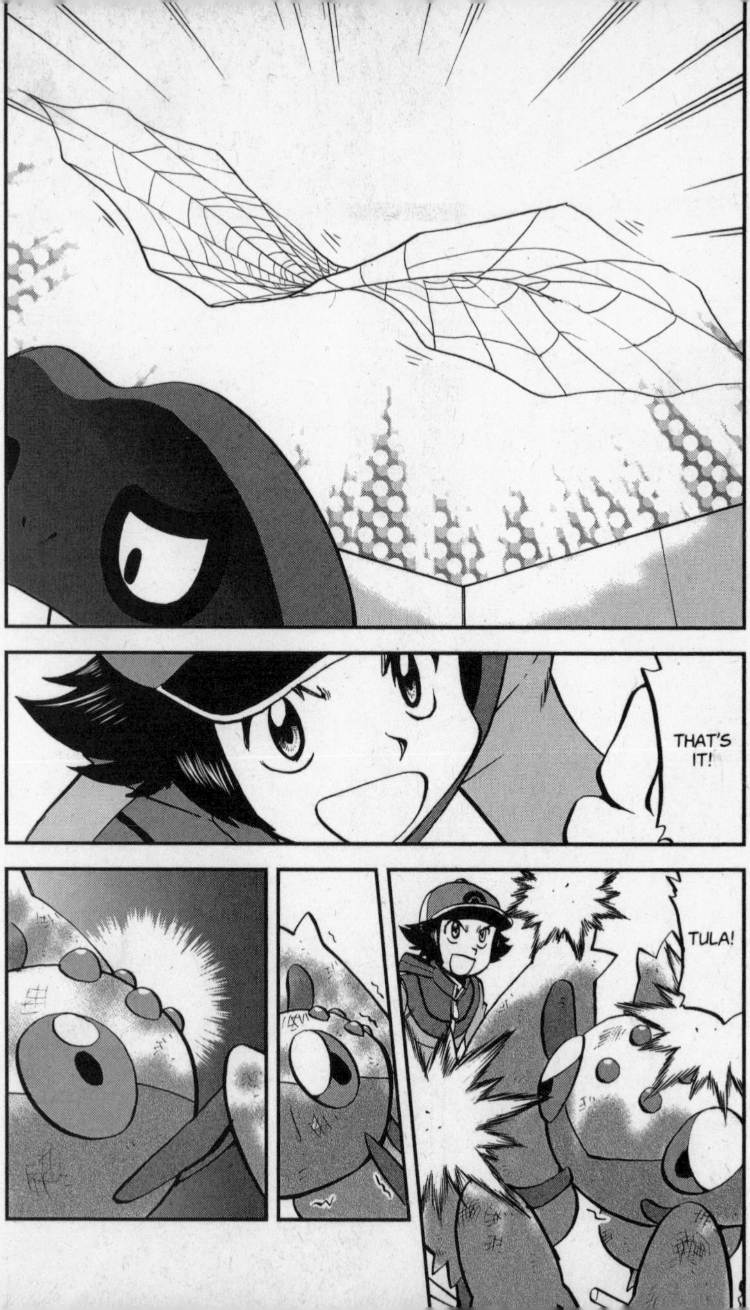
THAT'S IT!
TULA!

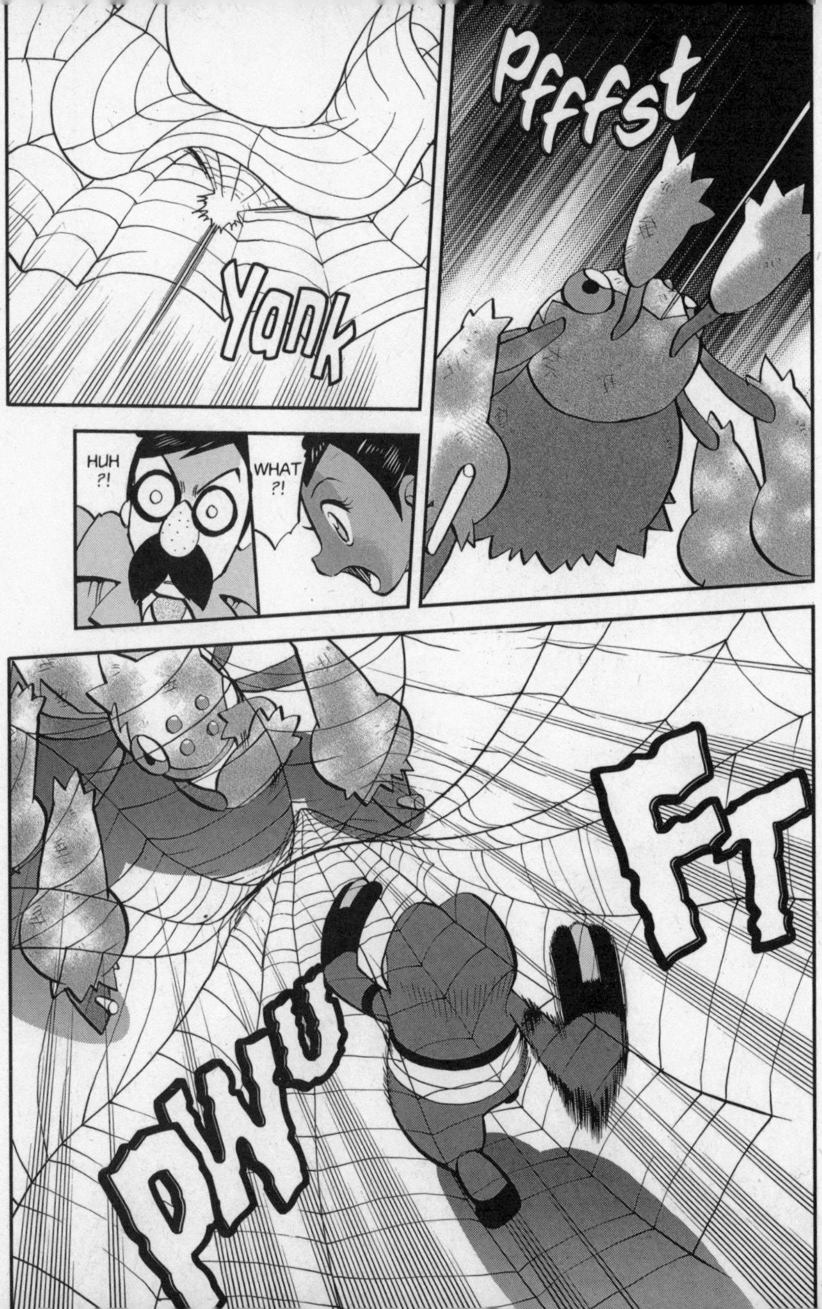
Pfffst
Yank
WHAT ?!
HUH ?!
PHUFT

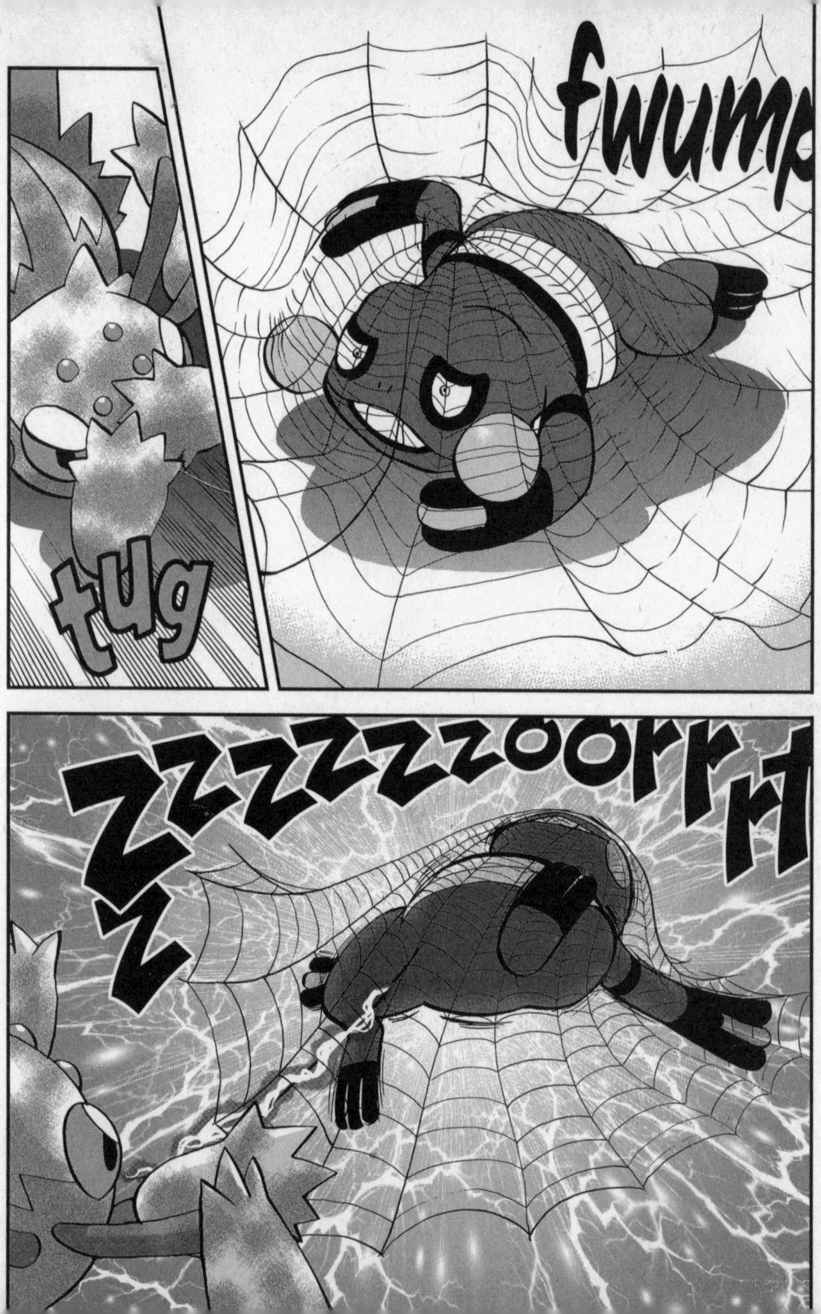
fwump
tug
ZZZZZZOOrrrt

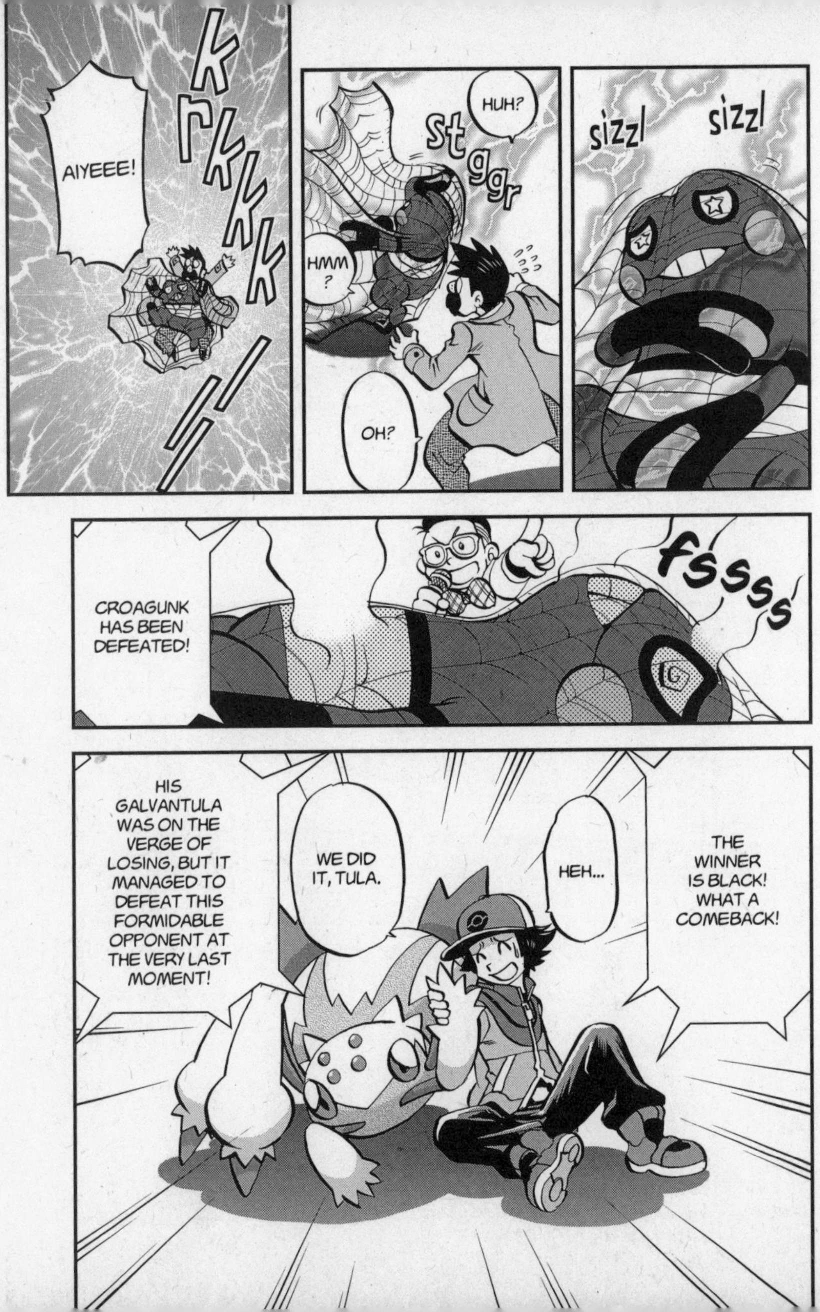
sizzl
sizzl
HUH?
stggr
HMM?
OH?
AIYEEE!
krkkkk
fssss
CROAGUNK HAS BEEN DEFEATED!
THE WINNER IS BLACK! WHAT A COMEBACK!
HEH...
WE DID IT, TULA.
HIS GALVANTULA WAS ON THE VERGE OF LOSING, BUT IT MANAGED TO DEFEAT THIS FORMIDABLE OPPONENT AT THE VERY LAST MOMENT!

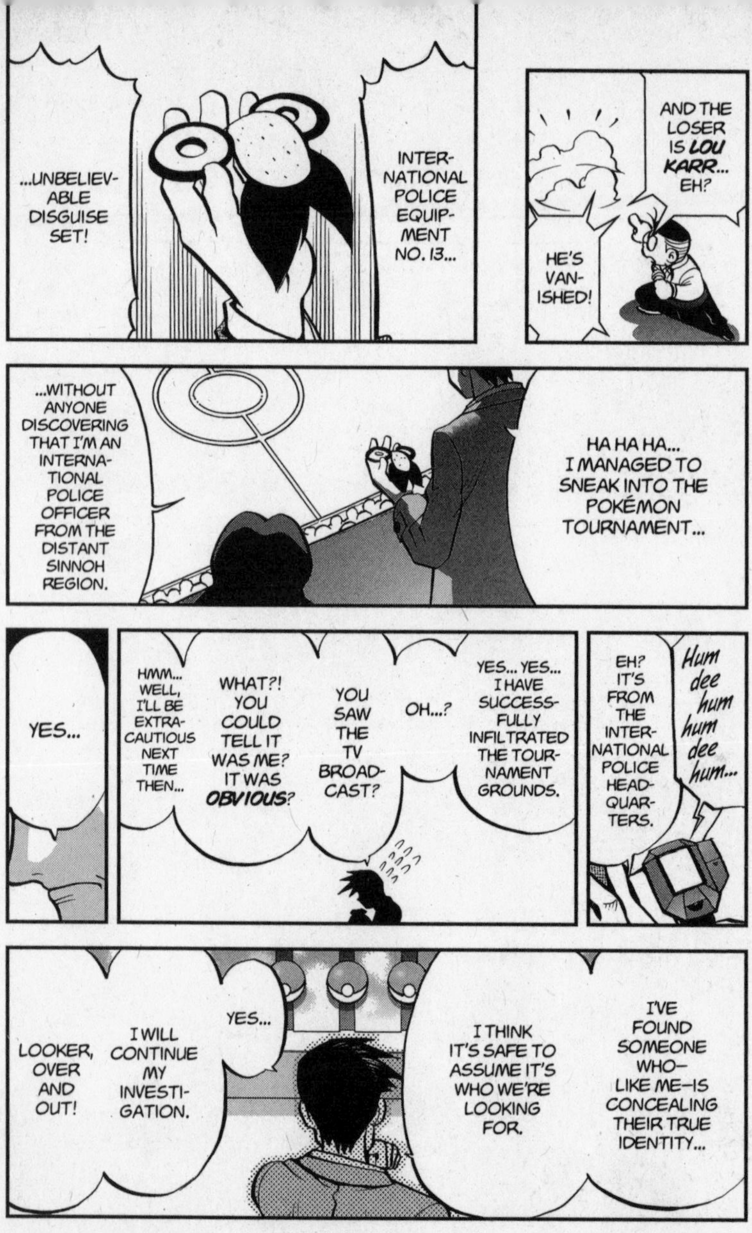
AND THE LOSER IS **LOU KARR**... EH?
HE'S VANISHED!
INTERNATIONAL POLICE EQUIPMENT NO. 13...
...UNBELIEVABLE DISGUISE SET!
HA HA HA... I MANAGED TO SNEAK INTO THE POKÉMON TOURNAMENT...
...WITHOUT ANYONE DISCOVERING THAT I'M AN INTERNATIONAL POLICE OFFICER FROM THE DISTANT SINNOH REGION.
Hum dee hum hum dee hum...
EH? IT'S FROM THE INTERNATIONAL POLICE HEADQUARTERS.
YES... YES... I HAVE SUCCESSFULLY INFILTRATED THE TOURNAMENT GROUNDS.
OH...?
YOU SAW THE TV BROADCAST?
WHAT?! YOU COULD TELL IT WAS ME? IT WAS ***OBVIOUS***?
HMM... WELL, I'LL BE EXTRA-CAUTIOUS NEXT TIME THEN...
YES...
I'VE FOUND SOMEONE WHO—LIKE ME—IS CONCEALING THEIR TRUE IDENTITY...
I THINK IT'S SAFE TO ASSUME IT'S WHO WE'RE LOOKING FOR.
YES...
I WILL CONTINUE MY INVESTIGATION.
LOOKER, OVER AND OUT!

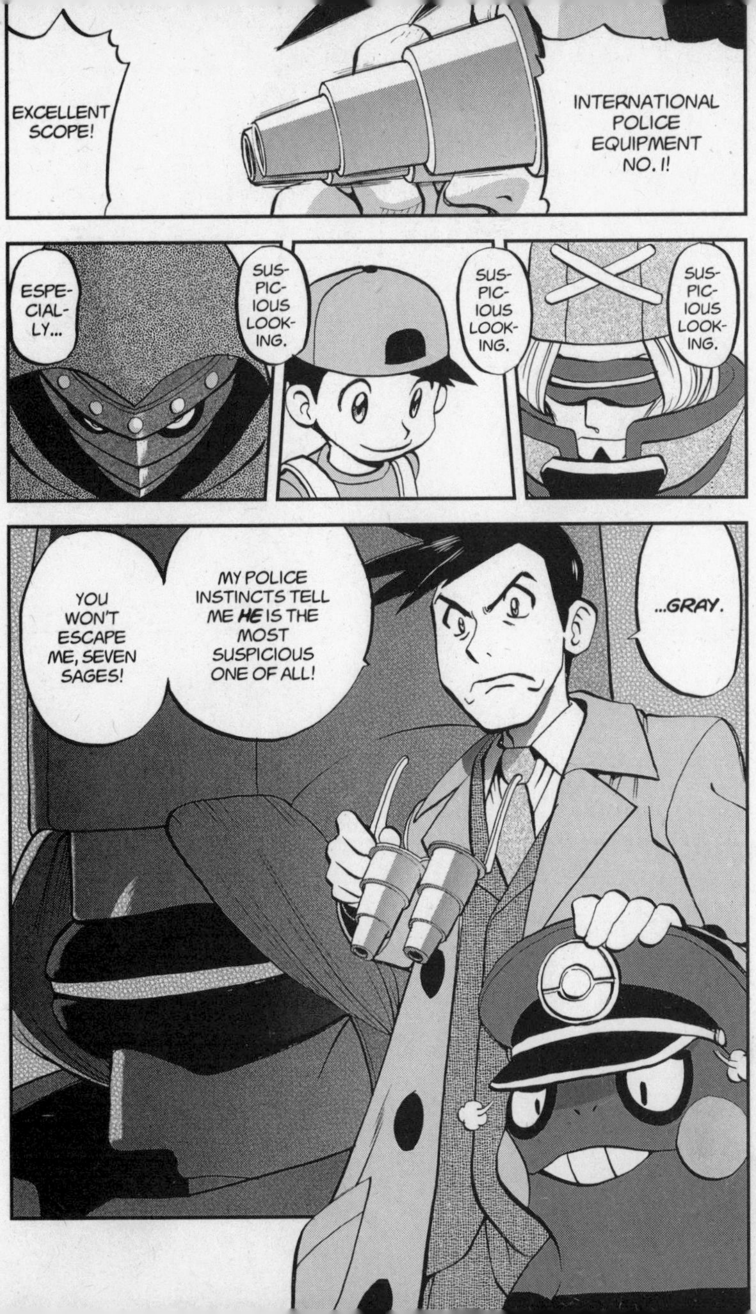
INTERNATIONAL POLICE EQUIPMENT NO. 1!
EXCELLENT SCOPE!
SUSPICIOUS LOOKING.
SUSPICIOUS LOOKING.
SUSPICIOUS LOOKING.
ESPECIALLY...
...GRAY.
MY POLICE INSTINCTS TELL ME **HE** IS THE MOST SUSPICIOUS ONE OF ALL!
YOU WON'T ESCAPE ME, SEVEN SAGES!

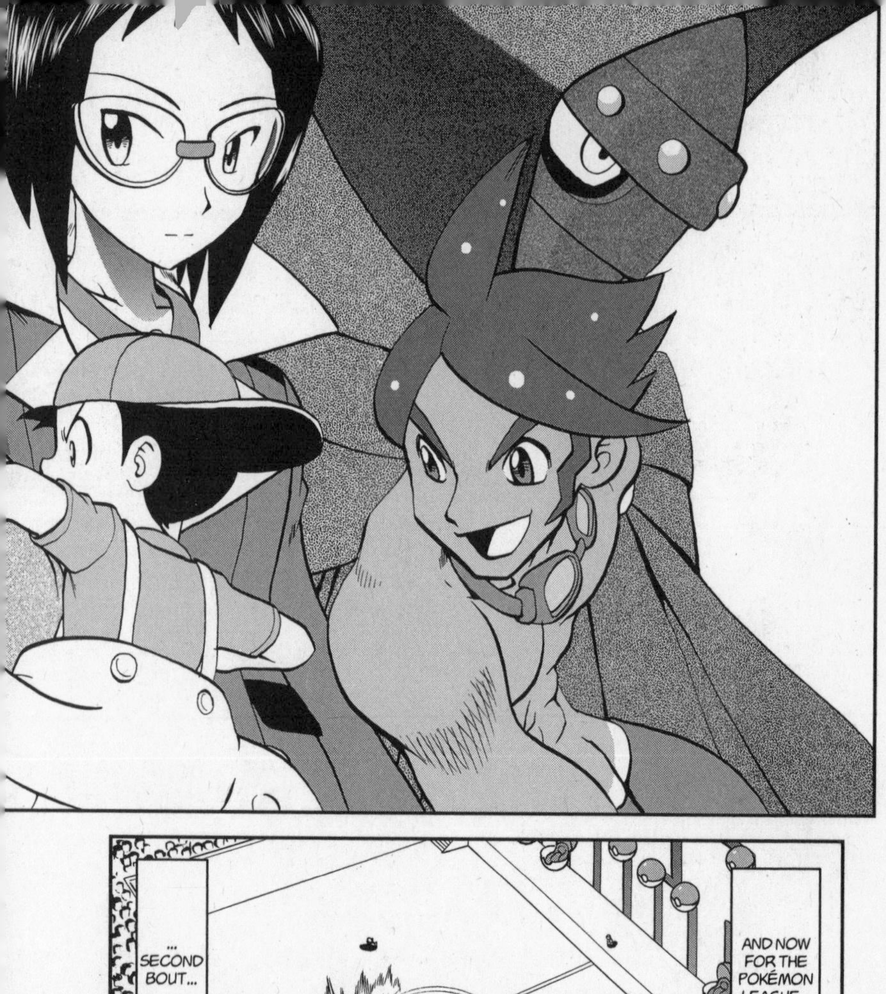

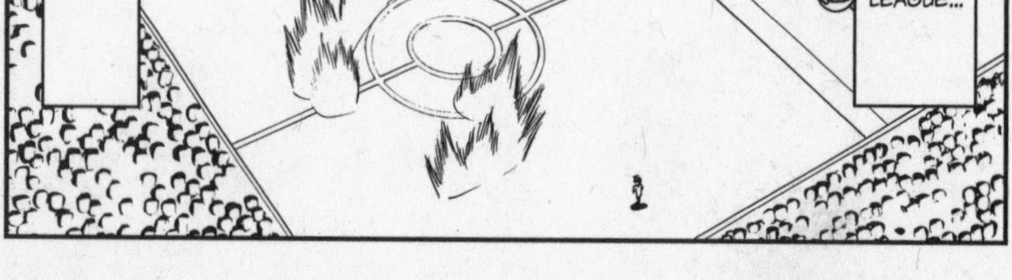
AND NOW FOR THE POKÉMON LEAGUE...
...SECOND BOUT...

Adventure 56 The Tournament Continues

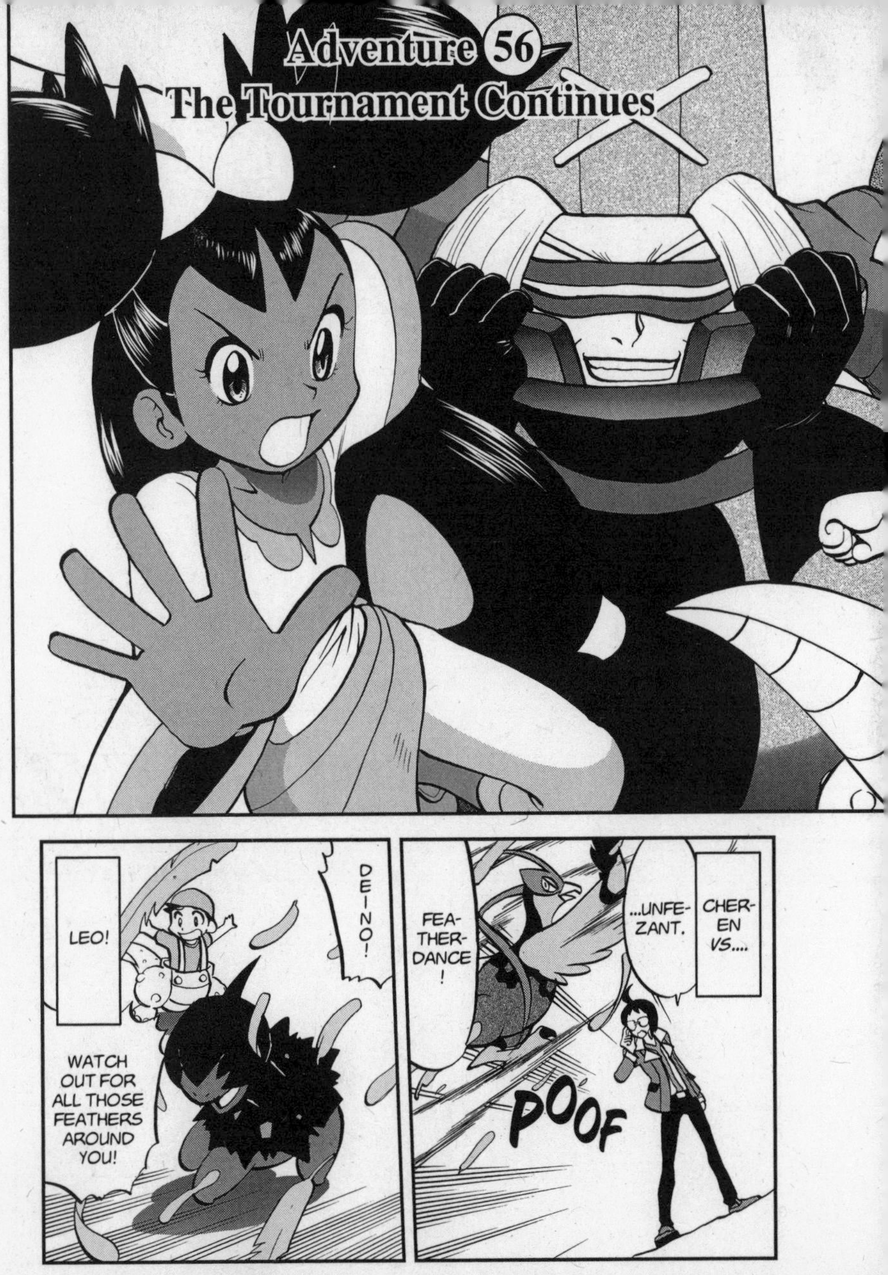

CHER-EN VS....
...UNFE-ZANT.
FEA-THER-DANCE!
POOF
DE-I-NO!
LEO!
WATCH OUT FOR ALL THOSE FEATHERS AROUND YOU!

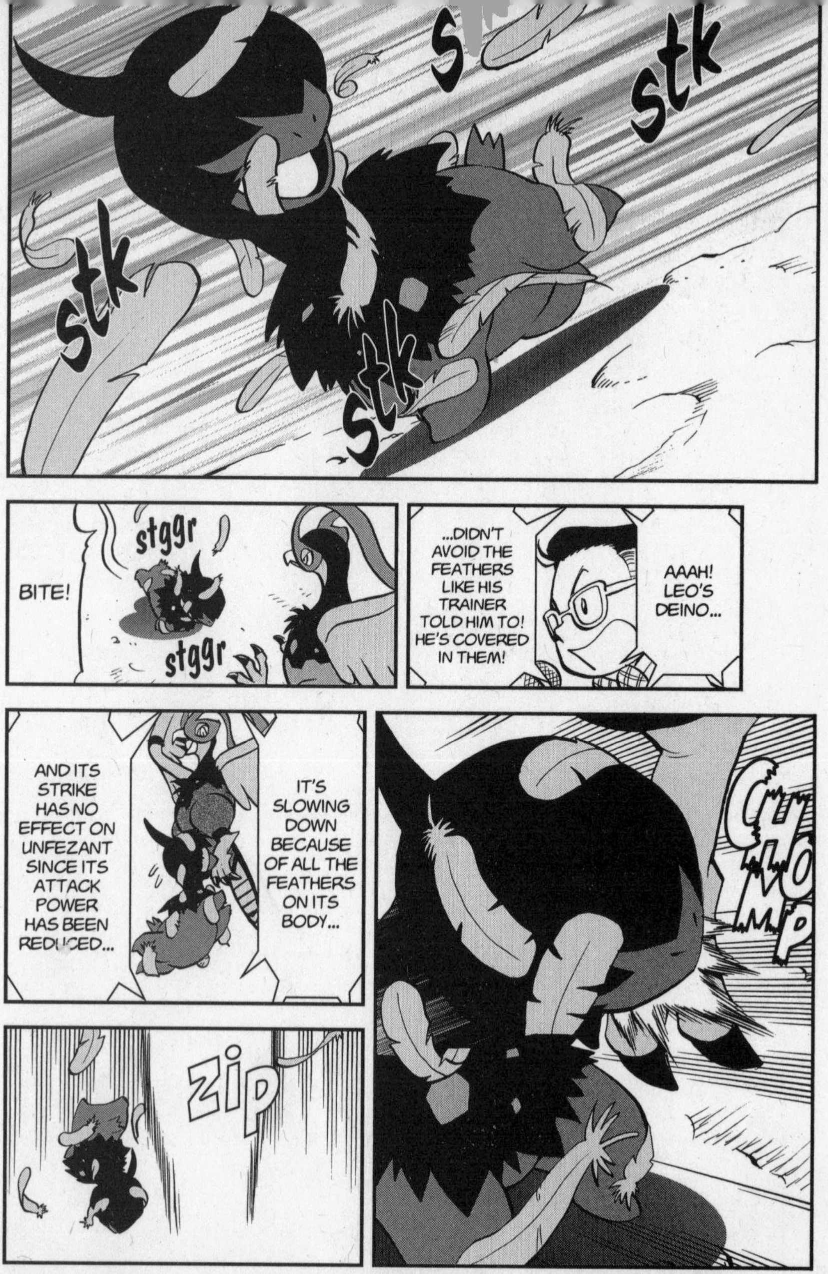
stk
stk
stk
AAAH! LEO'S DEINO...
...DIDN'T AVOID THE FEATHERS LIKE HIS TRAINER TOLD HIM TO! HE'S COVERED IN THEM!
stggr
BITE!
stggr
CHOMP
IT'S SLOWING DOWN BECAUSE OF ALL THE FEATHERS ON ITS BODY...
AND ITS STRIKE HAS NO EFFECT ON UNFEZANT SINCE ITS ATTACK POWER HAS BEEN REDUCED...
zip

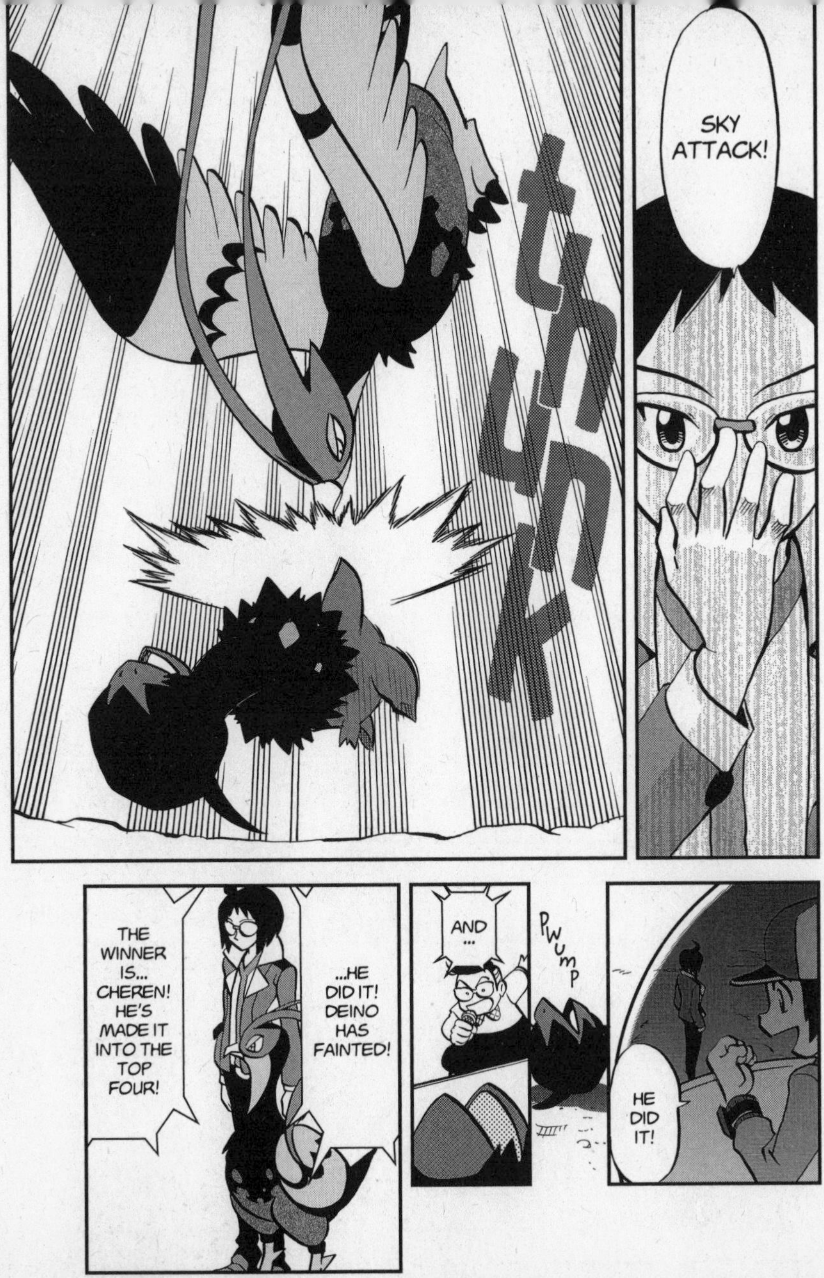
SKY ATTACK!
THUNK
HE DID IT!
AND ...
PWUMP
...HE DID IT! DEINO HAS FAINTED!
THE WINNER IS... CHEREN! HE'S MADE IT INTO THE TOP FOUR!

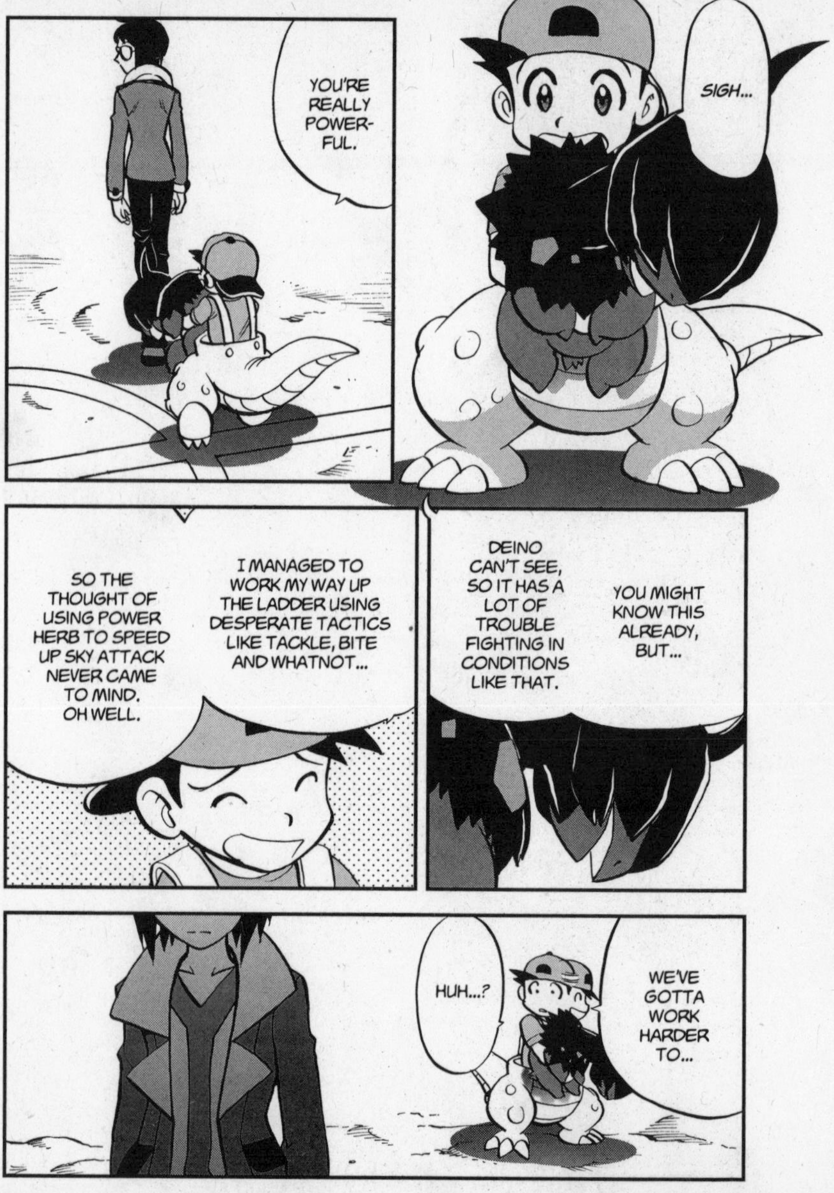
SIGH...
YOU'RE REALLY POWER-FUL.
YOU MIGHT KNOW THIS ALREADY, BUT...
DEINO CAN'T SEE, SO IT HAS A LOT OF TROUBLE FIGHTING IN CONDITIONS LIKE THAT.
I MANAGED TO WORK MY WAY UP THE LADDER USING DESPERATE TACTICS LIKE TACKLE, BITE AND WHATNOT...
SO THE THOUGHT OF USING POWER HERB TO SPEED UP SKY ATTACK NEVER CAME TO MIND. OH WELL.
WE'VE GOTTA WORK HARDER TO...
HUH...?

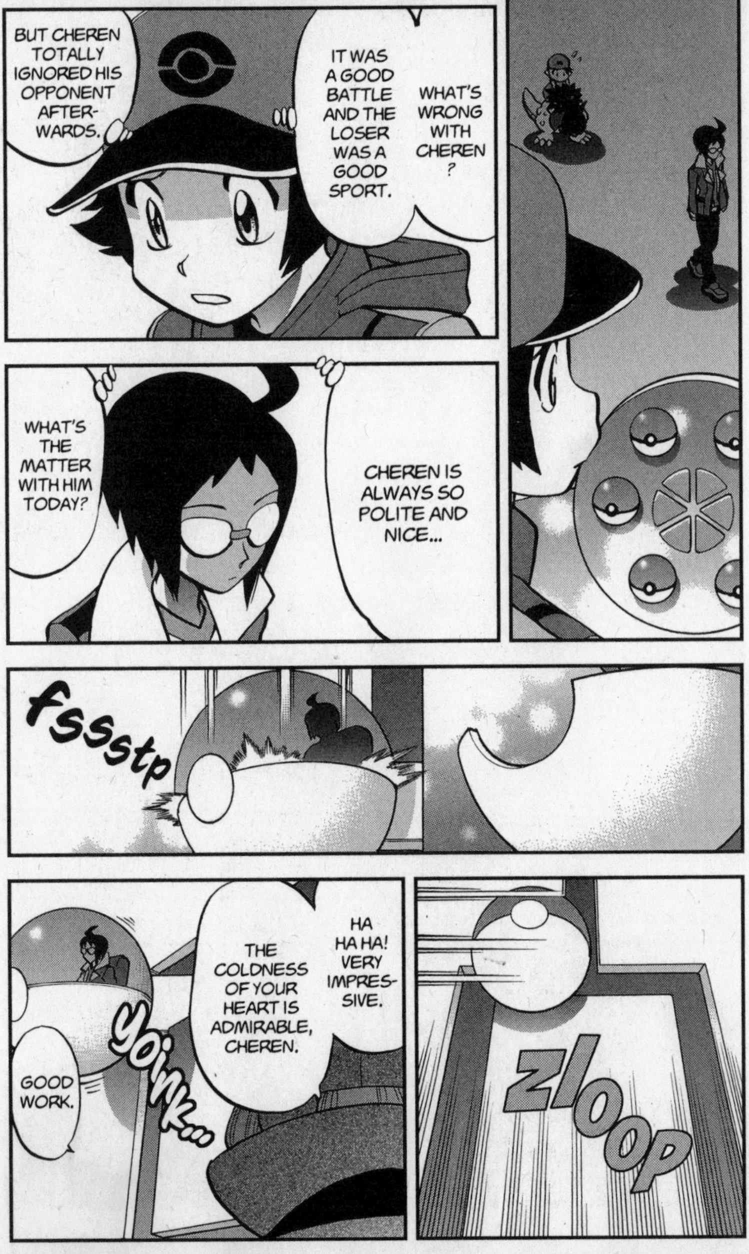
WHAT'S WRONG WITH CHEREN?
IT WAS A GOOD BATTLE AND THE LOSER WAS A GOOD SPORT.
BUT CHEREN TOTALLY IGNORED HIS OPPONENT AFTER-WARDS.
CHEREN IS ALWAYS SO POLITE AND NICE...
WHAT'S THE MATTER WITH HIM TODAY?
fssstp
ZIOOP
HA HA HA! VERY IMPRES-SIVE.
THE COLDNESS OF YOUR HEART IS ADMIRABLE, CHEREN.
yoink...
GOOD WORK.

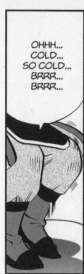

COOLNESS, COLDNESS...
THAT IS THE ESSENCE OF LIFE.
OHHH... COLD... SO COLD... BRRR... BRRR...
HEH HEH HEH HEH...
SO COLD. SO COLD.
HEH HEH HEH HEH...
SO COLD. SO COLD.
HM...

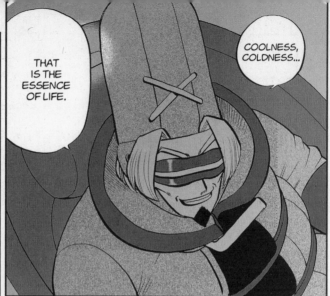

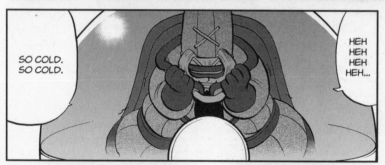

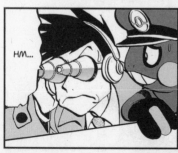

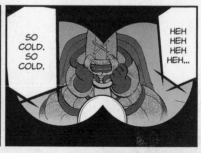

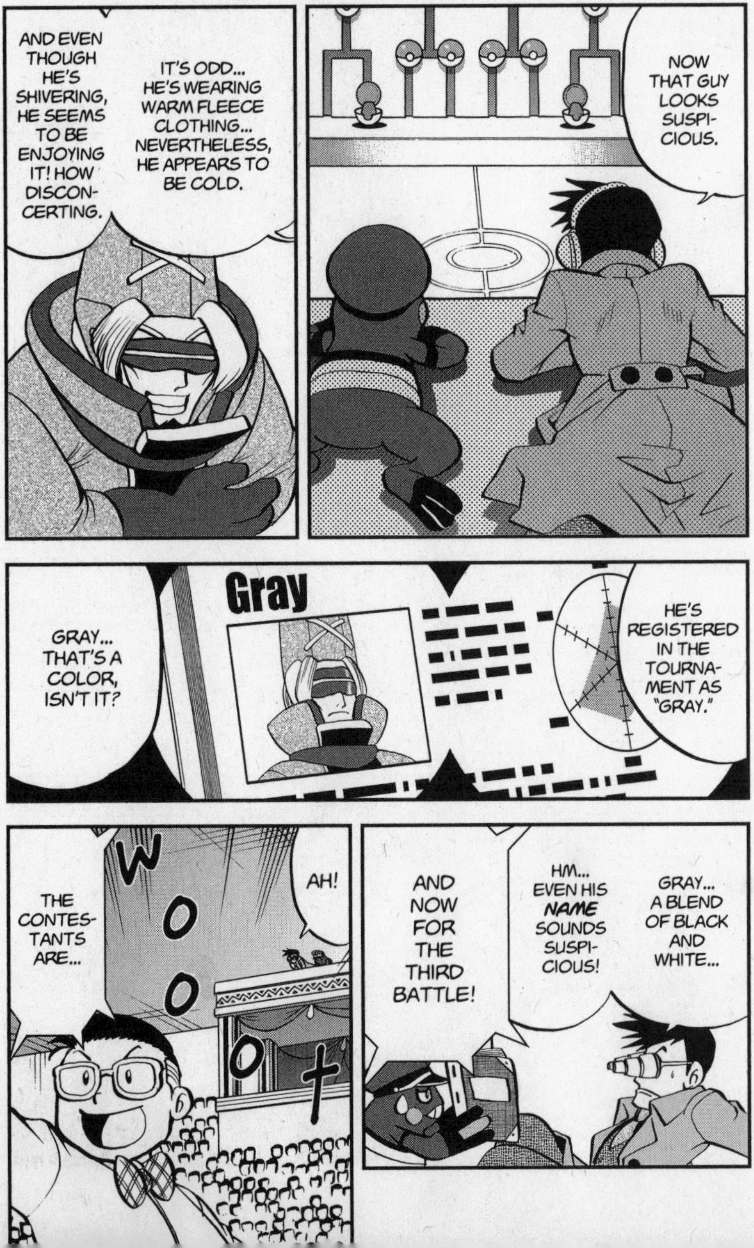
NOW THAT GUY LOOKS SUSPICIOUS.
IT'S ODD... HE'S WEARING WARM FLEECE CLOTHING... NEVERTHELESS, HE APPEARS TO BE COLD.
AND EVEN THOUGH HE'S SHIVERING, HE SEEMS TO BE ENJOYING IT! HOW DISCONCERTING.
HE'S REGISTERED IN THE TOURNAMENT AS "GRAY."
Gray
GRAY... THAT'S A COLOR, ISN'T IT?
GRAY... A BLEND OF BLACK AND WHITE...
HM... EVEN HIS *NAME* SOUNDS SUSPICIOUS!
AND NOW FOR THE THIRD BATTLE!
AH!
WOOOOT
THE CONTESTANTS ARE...

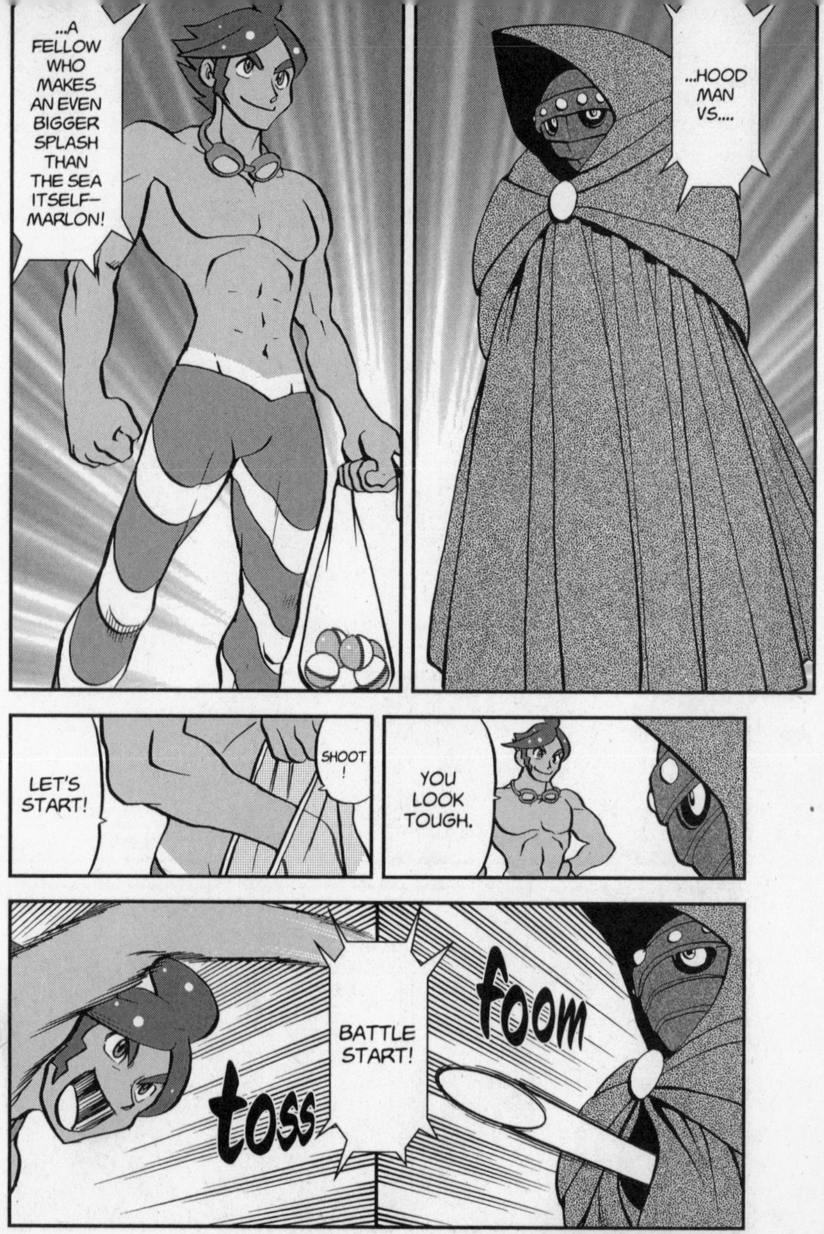
...HOOD MAN VS....
...A FELLOW WHO MAKES AN EVEN BIGGER SPLASH THAN THE SEA ITSELF—MARLON!
YOU LOOK TOUGH.
SHOOT !
LET'S START!
foom
BATTLE START!
toss

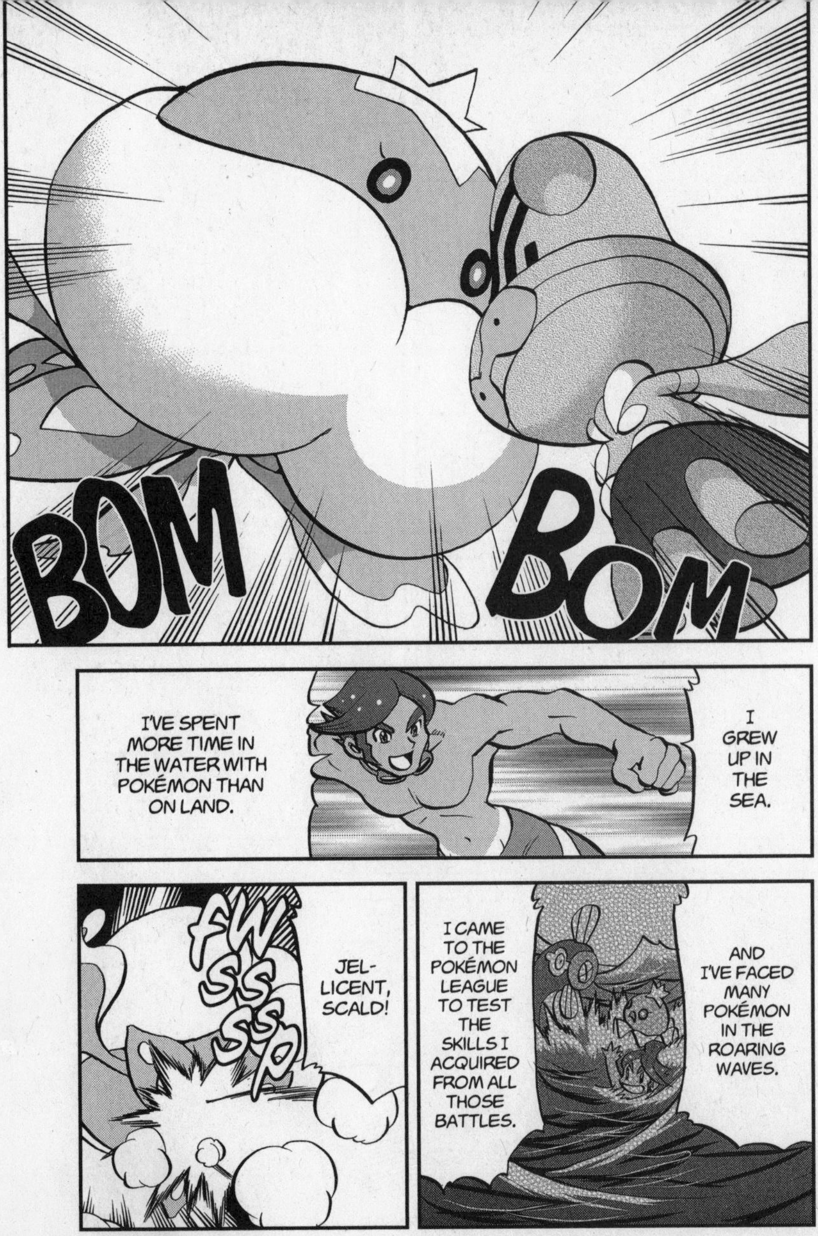
BOM
BOM
I GREW UP IN THE SEA.
I'VE SPENT MORE TIME IN THE WATER WITH POKÉMON THAN ON LAND.
AND I'VE FACED MANY POKÉMON IN THE ROARING WAVES.
I CAME TO THE POKÉMON LEAGUE TO TEST THE SKILLS I ACQUIRED FROM ALL THOSE BATTLES.
JEL-LICENT, SCALD!
FWSSSSP

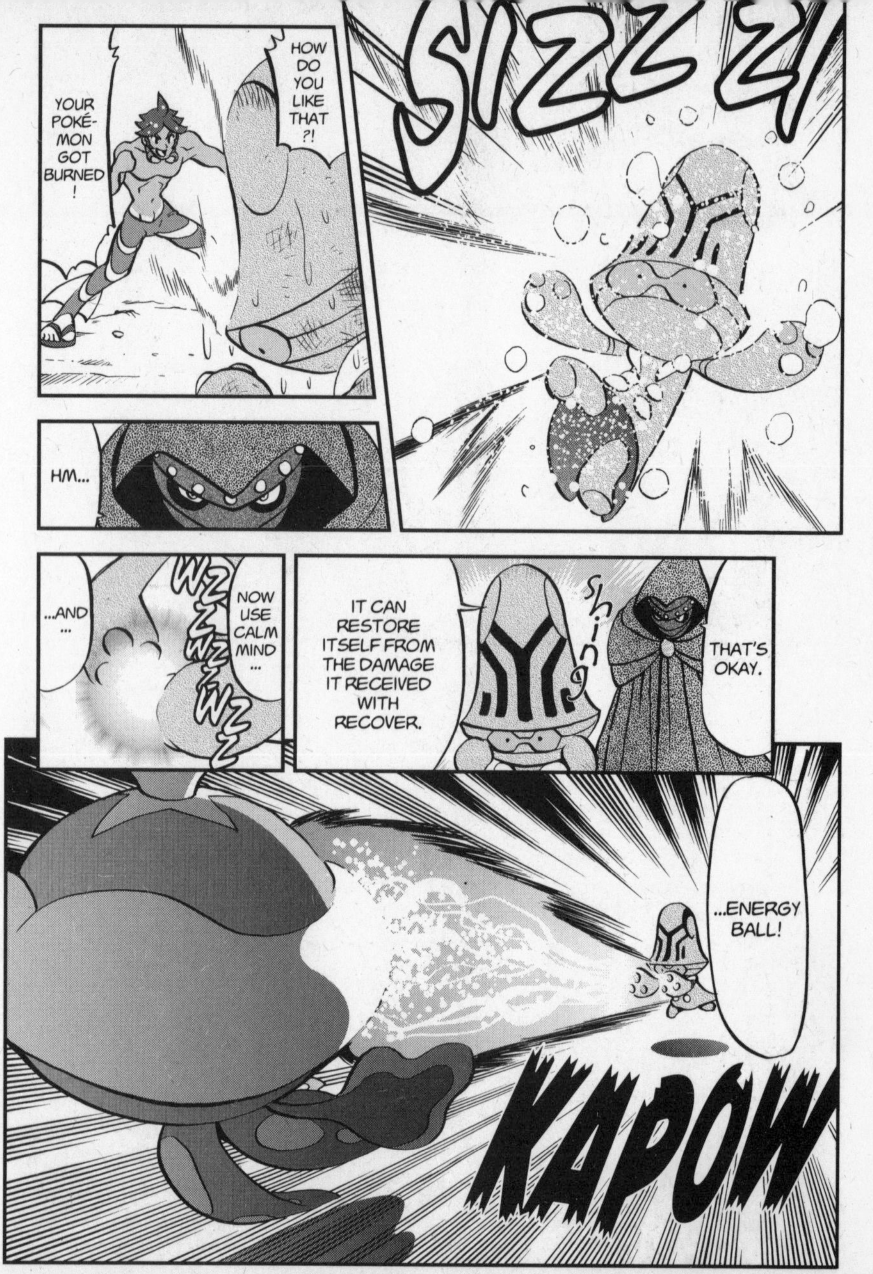
SIZZZ!
HOW DO YOU LIKE THAT?!
YOUR POKÉMON GOT BURNED!
HM...
THAT'S OKAY.
IT CAN RESTORE ITSELF FROM THE DAMAGE IT RECEIVED WITH RECOVER.
shing
NOW USE CALM MIND...
WZZZZZ
...AND...
...ENERGY BALL!
KAPOW

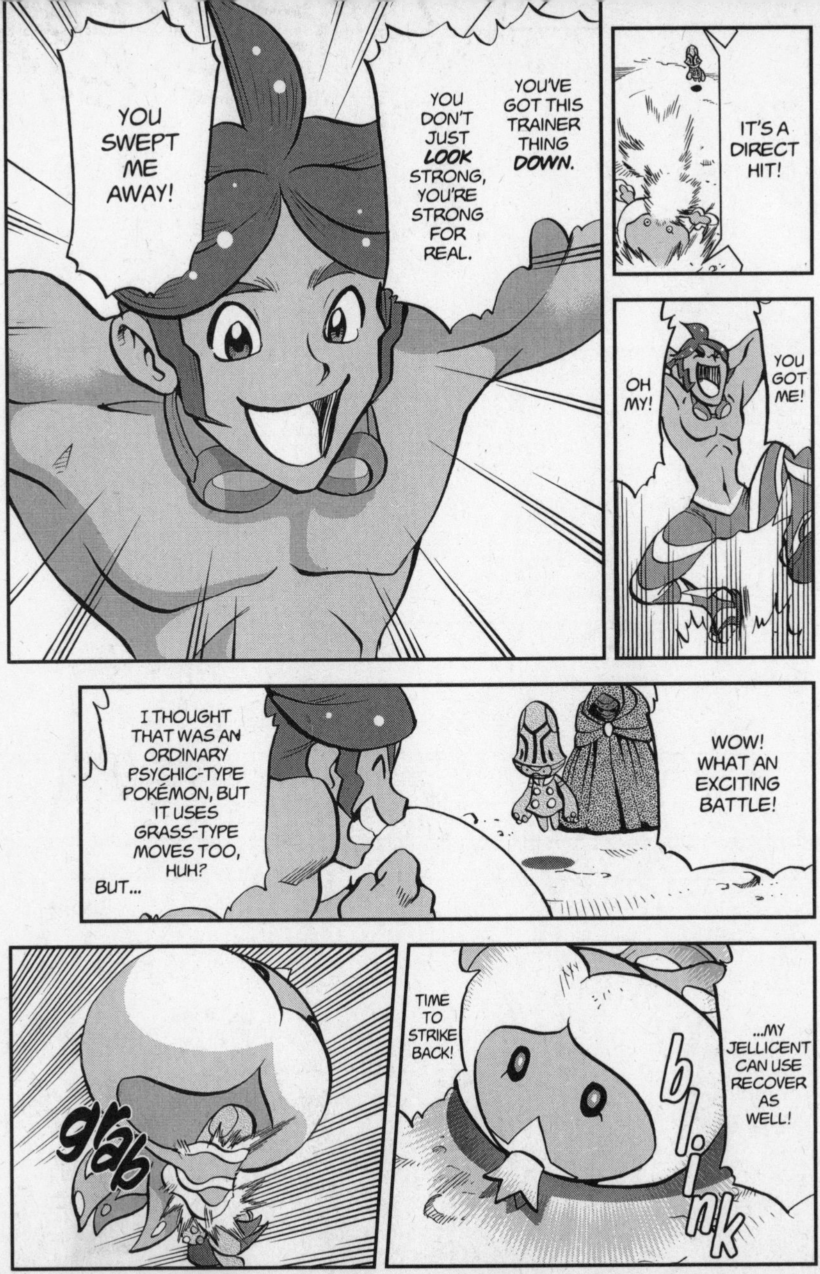
IT'S A DIRECT HIT!
YOU GOT ME!
OH MY!
YOU'VE GOT THIS TRAINER THING **DOWN**.
YOU DON'T JUST **LOOK** STRONG, YOU'RE STRONG FOR REAL.
YOU SWEPT ME AWAY!
WOW! WHAT AN EXCITING BATTLE!
I THOUGHT THAT WAS AN ORDINARY PSYCHIC-TYPE POKÉMON, BUT IT USES GRASS-TYPE MOVES TOO, HUH?
BUT...
...MY JELLICENT CAN USE RECOVER AS WELL!
blink
TIME TO STRIKE BACK!
grab

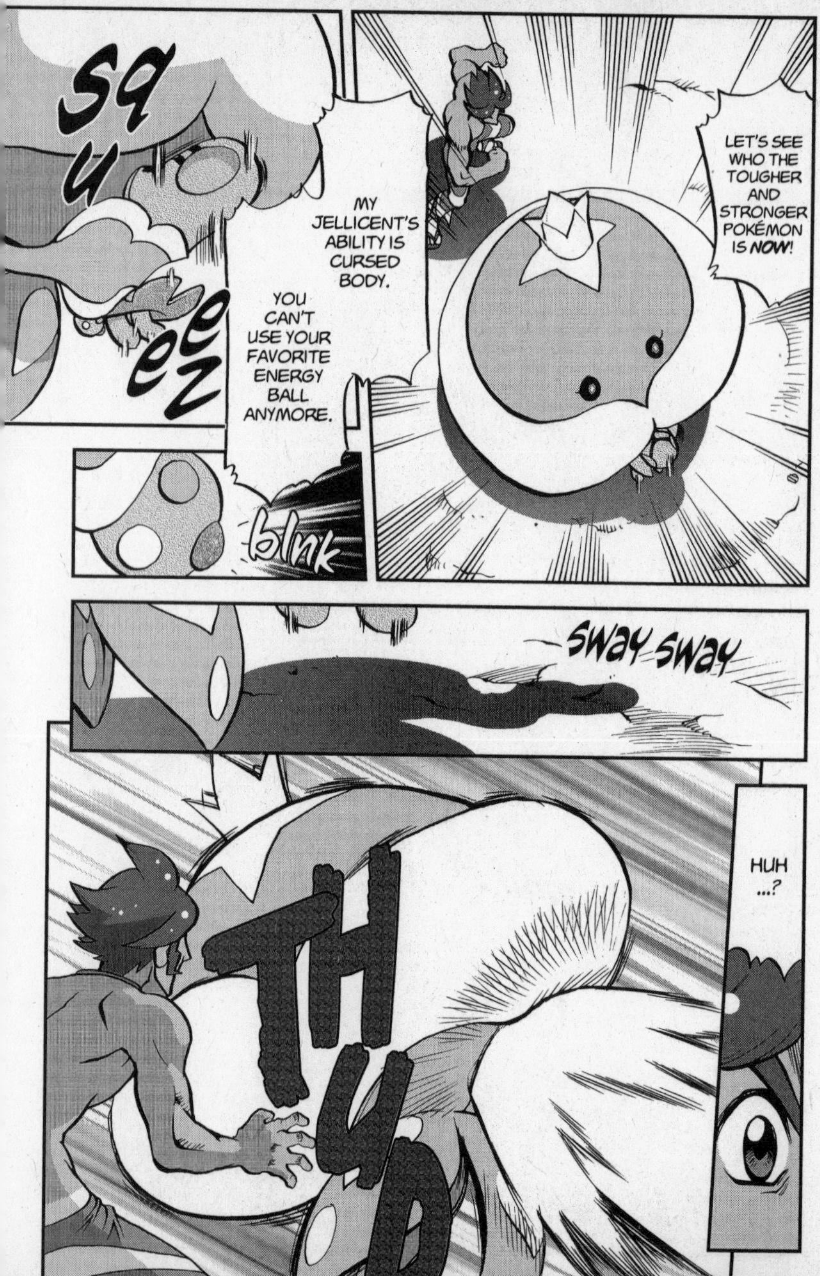
LET'S SEE WHO THE TOUGHER AND STRONGER POKÉMON IS NOW!
MY JELLICENT'S ABILITY IS CURSED BODY.
YOU CAN'T USE YOUR FAVORITE ENERGY BALL ANYMORE.
squeeze
blink
sway sway
HUH ...?
THUD

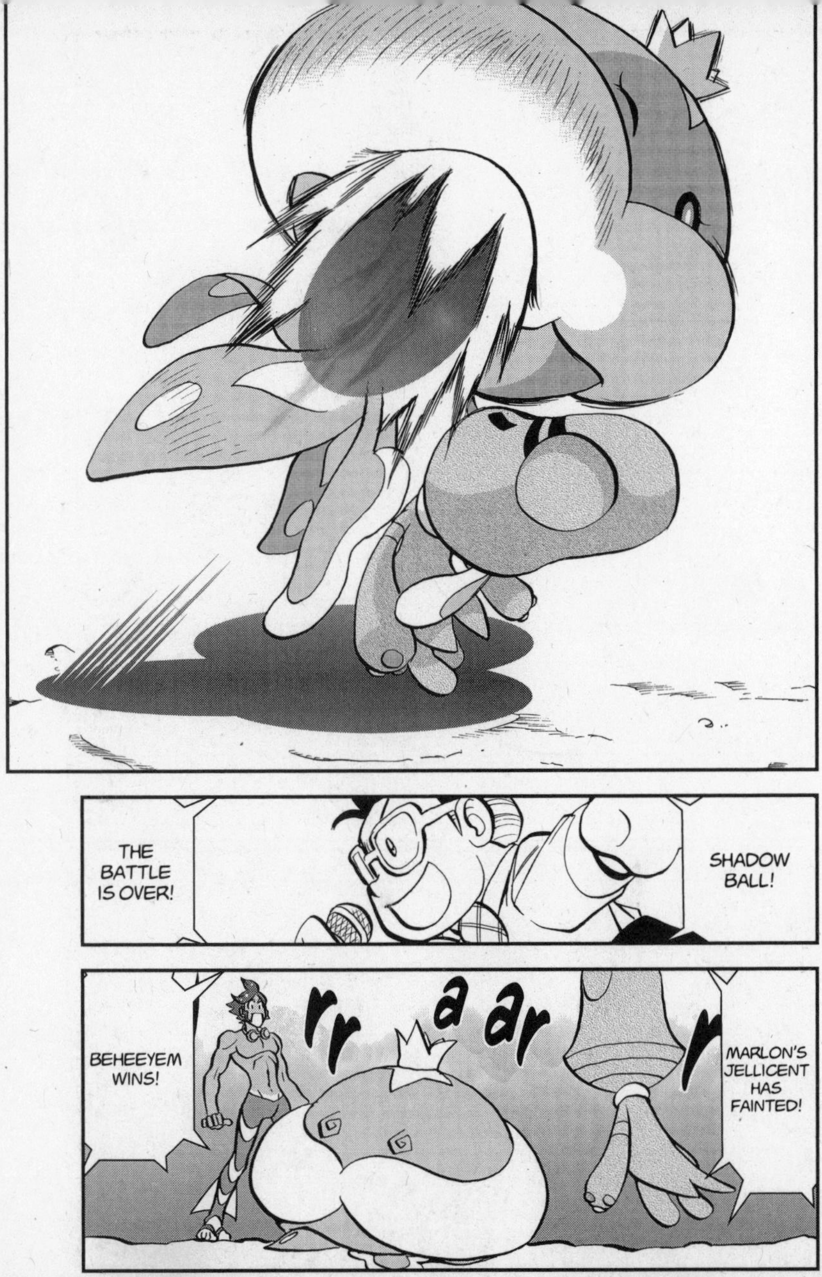
SHADOW BALL!
THE BATTLE IS OVER!
MARLON'S JELLICENT HAS FAINTED!
rr a ar r
BEHEEYEM WINS!

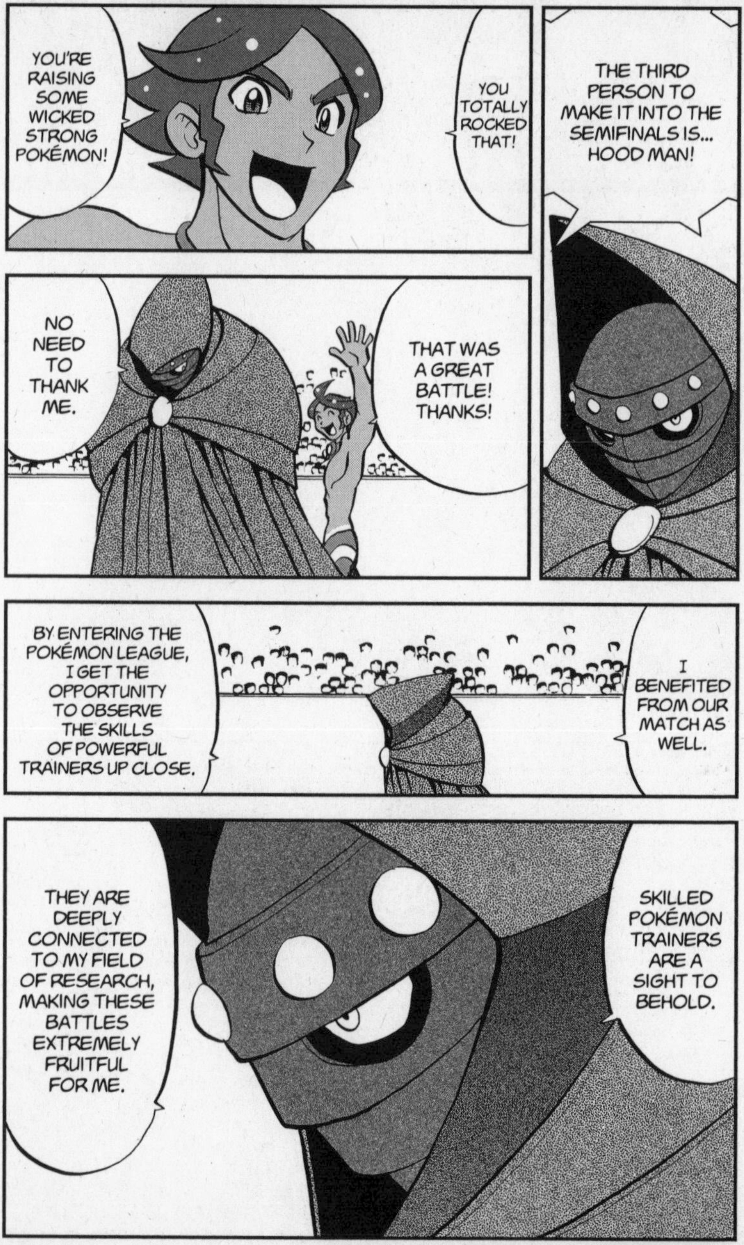
THE THIRD PERSON TO MAKE IT INTO THE SEMIFINALS IS... HOOD MAN!
YOU TOTALLY ROCKED THAT!
YOU'RE RAISING SOME WICKED STRONG POKÉMON!
THAT WAS A GREAT BATTLE! THANKS!
NO NEED TO THANK ME.
I BENEFITED FROM OUR MATCH AS WELL.
BY ENTERING THE POKÉMON LEAGUE, I GET THE OPPORTUNITY TO OBSERVE THE SKILLS OF POWERFUL TRAINERS UP CLOSE.
SKILLED POKÉMON TRAINERS ARE A SIGHT TO BEHOLD.
THEY ARE DEEPLY CONNECTED TO MY FIELD OF RESEARCH, MAKING THESE BATTLES EXTREMELY FRUITFUL FOR ME.

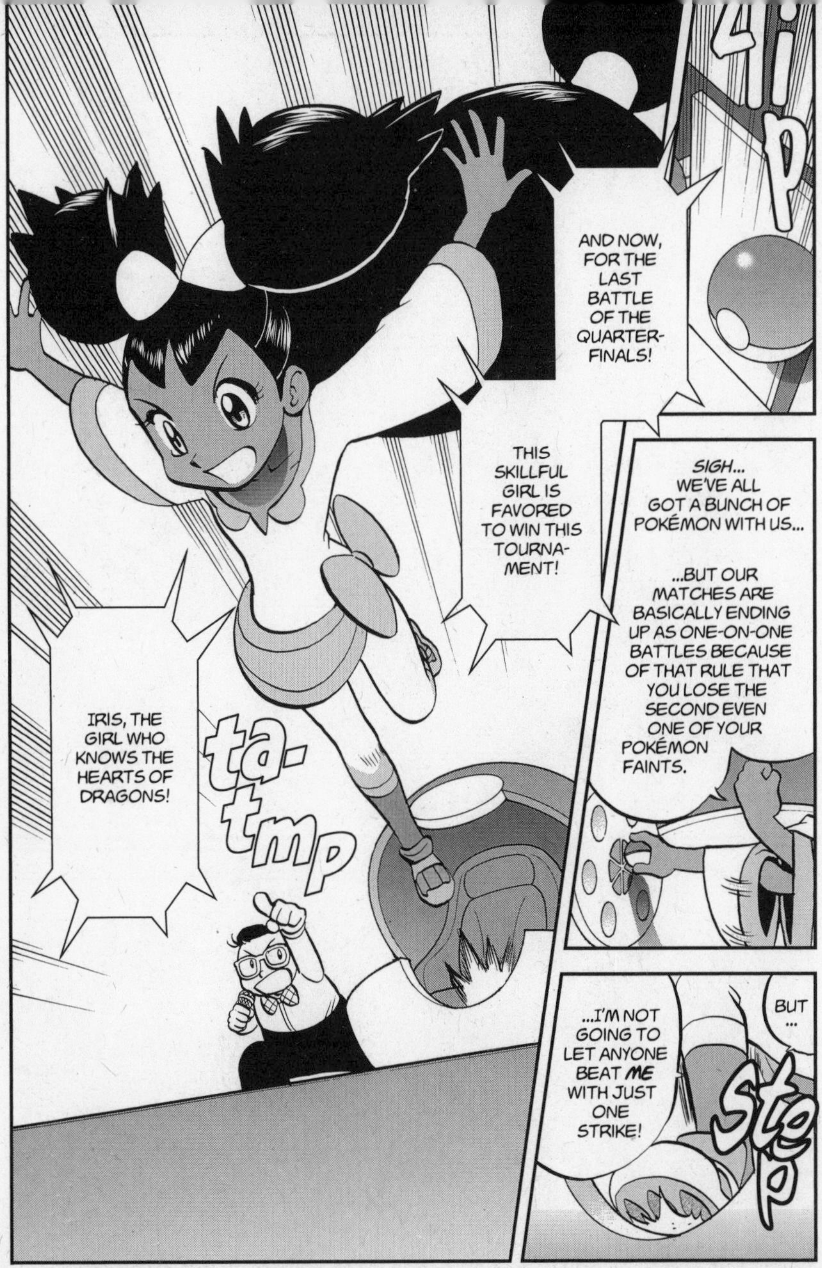
zip
AND NOW, FOR THE LAST BATTLE OF THE QUARTER-FINALS!
THIS SKILLFUL GIRL IS FAVORED TO WIN THIS TOURNA-MENT!
IRIS, THE GIRL WHO KNOWS THE HEARTS OF DRAGONS!
ta-tmp
SIGH... WE'VE ALL GOT A BUNCH OF POKÉMON WITH US...
...BUT OUR MATCHES ARE BASICALLY ENDING UP AS ONE-ON-ONE BATTLES BECAUSE OF THAT RULE THAT YOU LOSE THE SECOND EVEN ONE OF YOUR POKÉMON FAINTS.
BUT...
...I'M NOT GOING TO LET ANYONE BEAT *ME* WITH JUST ONE STRIKE!
step

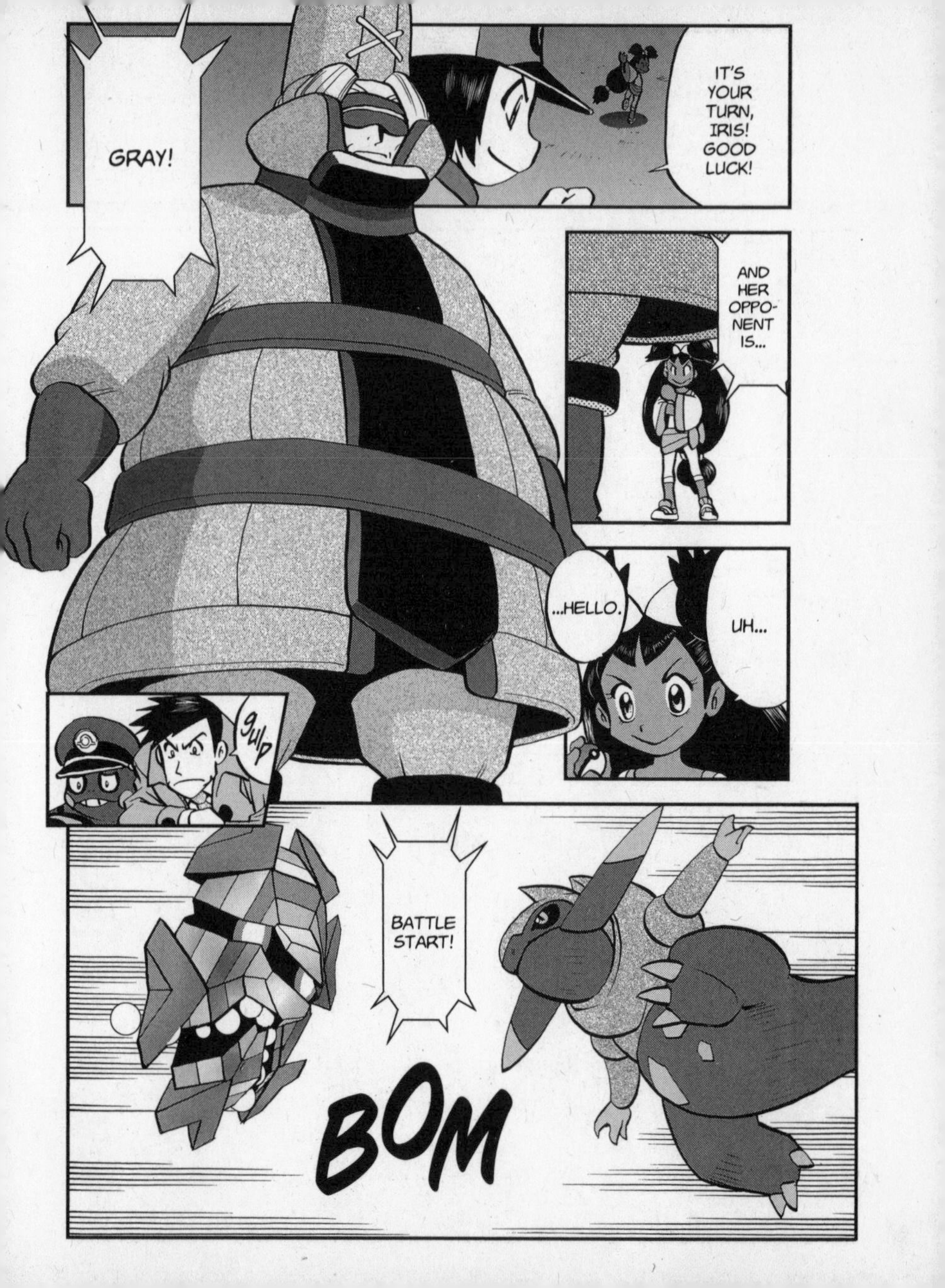
IT'S YOUR TURN, IRIS! GOOD LUCK!
GRAY!
AND HER OPPONENT IS...
UH...
...HELLO.
gulp
BATTLE START!
BOM

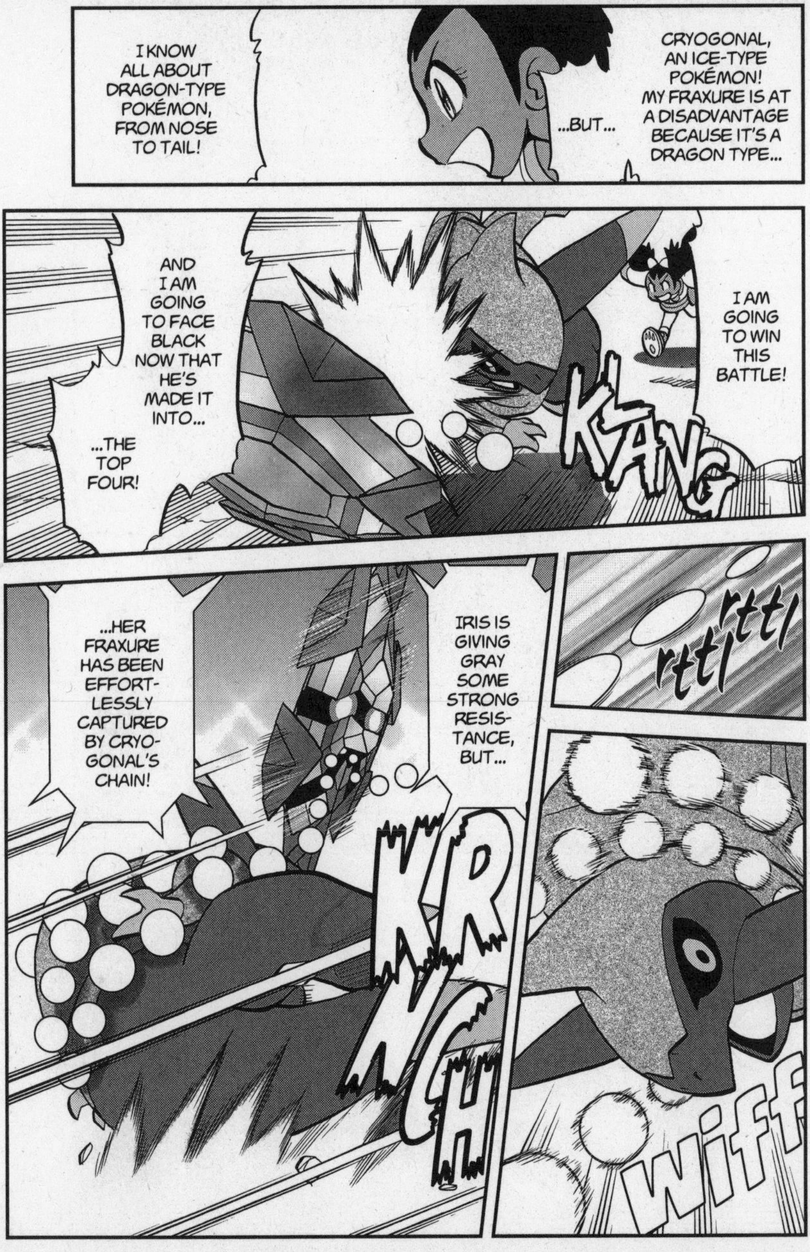
CRYOGONAL, AN ICE-TYPE POKÉMON! MY FRAXURE IS AT A DISADVANTAGE BECAUSE IT'S A DRAGON TYPE...
...BUT...
I KNOW ALL ABOUT DRAGON-TYPE POKÉMON, FROM NOSE TO TAIL!
I AM GOING TO WIN THIS BATTLE!
KLANG
AND I AM GOING TO FACE BLACK NOW THAT HE'S MADE IT INTO...
...THE TOP FOUR!
rttl rttl
wiff
IRIS IS GIVING GRAY SOME STRONG RESIS-TANCE, BUT...
...HER FRAXURE HAS BEEN EFFORT-LESSLY CAPTURED BY CRYO-GONAL'S CHAIN!
KRNCH

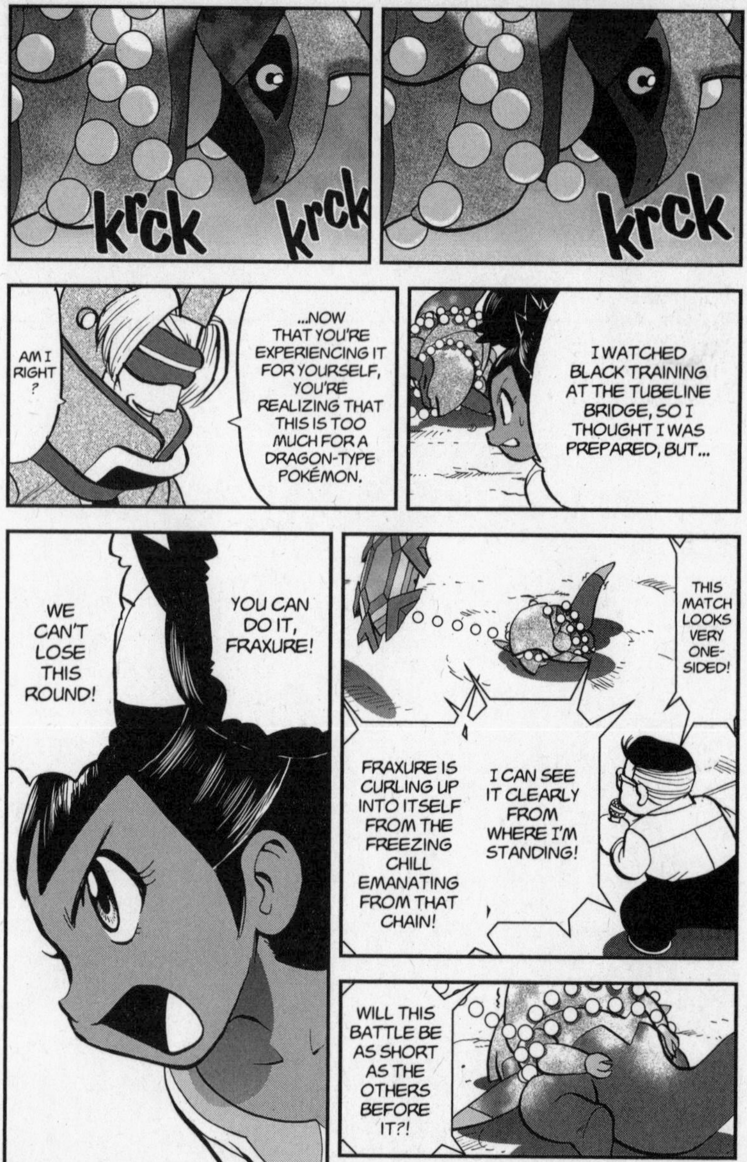
krck
krck
krck
I WATCHED BLACK TRAINING AT THE TUBELINE BRIDGE, SO I THOUGHT I WAS PREPARED, BUT...
...NOW THAT YOU'RE EXPERIENCING IT FOR YOURSELF, YOU'RE REALIZING THAT THIS IS TOO MUCH FOR A DRAGON-TYPE POKÉMON.
AM I RIGHT?
THIS MATCH LOOKS VERY ONE-SIDED!
I CAN SEE IT CLEARLY FROM WHERE I'M STANDING!
FRAXURE IS CURLING UP INTO ITSELF FROM THE FREEZING CHILL EMANATING FROM THAT CHAIN!
WILL THIS BATTLE BE AS SHORT AS THE OTHERS BEFORE IT?!
YOU CAN DO IT, FRAXURE!
WE CAN'T LOSE THIS ROUND!

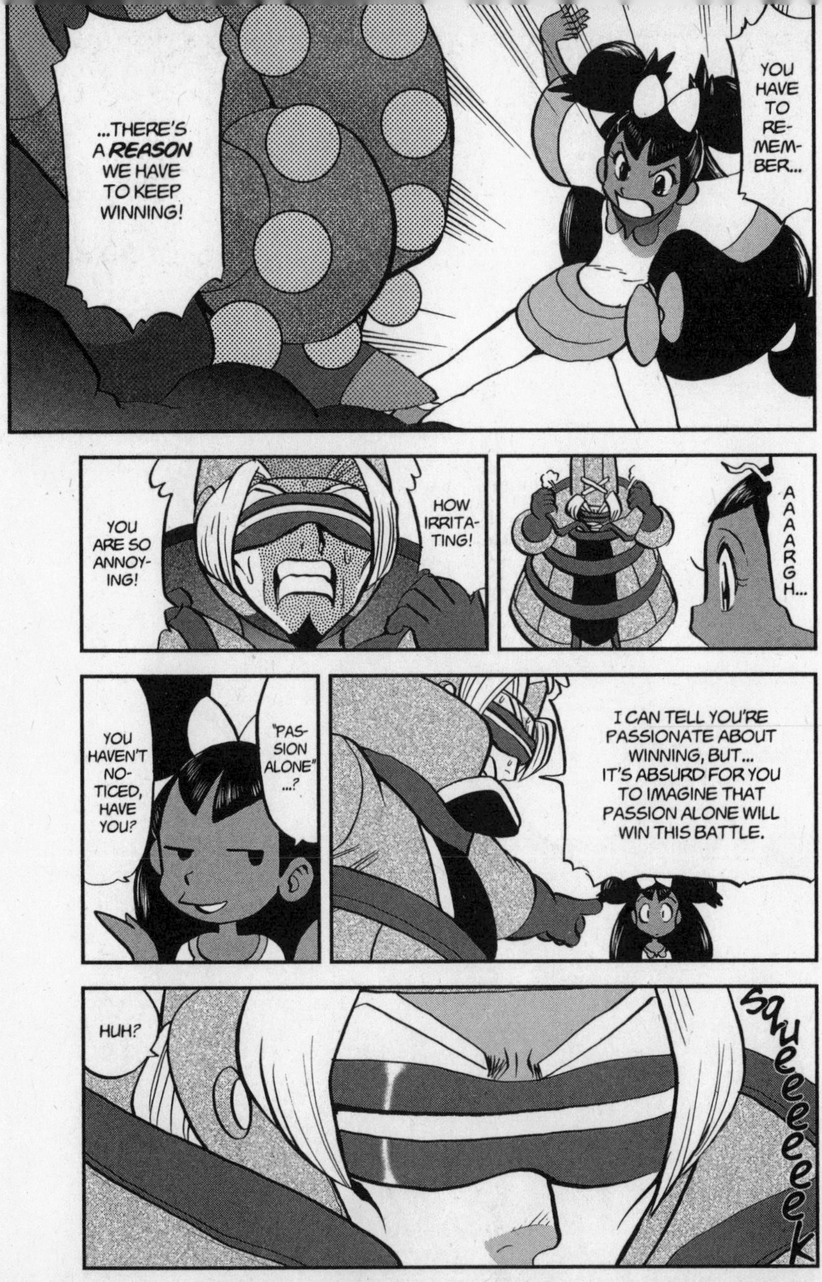
YOU HAVE TO REMEMBER...
...THERE'S A **REASON** WE HAVE TO KEEP WINNING!
AAAAARGH...
HOW IRRITATING!
YOU ARE SO ANNOYING!
I CAN TELL YOU'RE PASSIONATE ABOUT WINNING, BUT... IT'S ABSURD FOR YOU TO IMAGINE THAT PASSION ALONE WILL WIN THIS BATTLE.
"PASSION ALONE" ...?
YOU HAVEN'T NOTICED, HAVE YOU?
Squeeeeeeek
HUH?

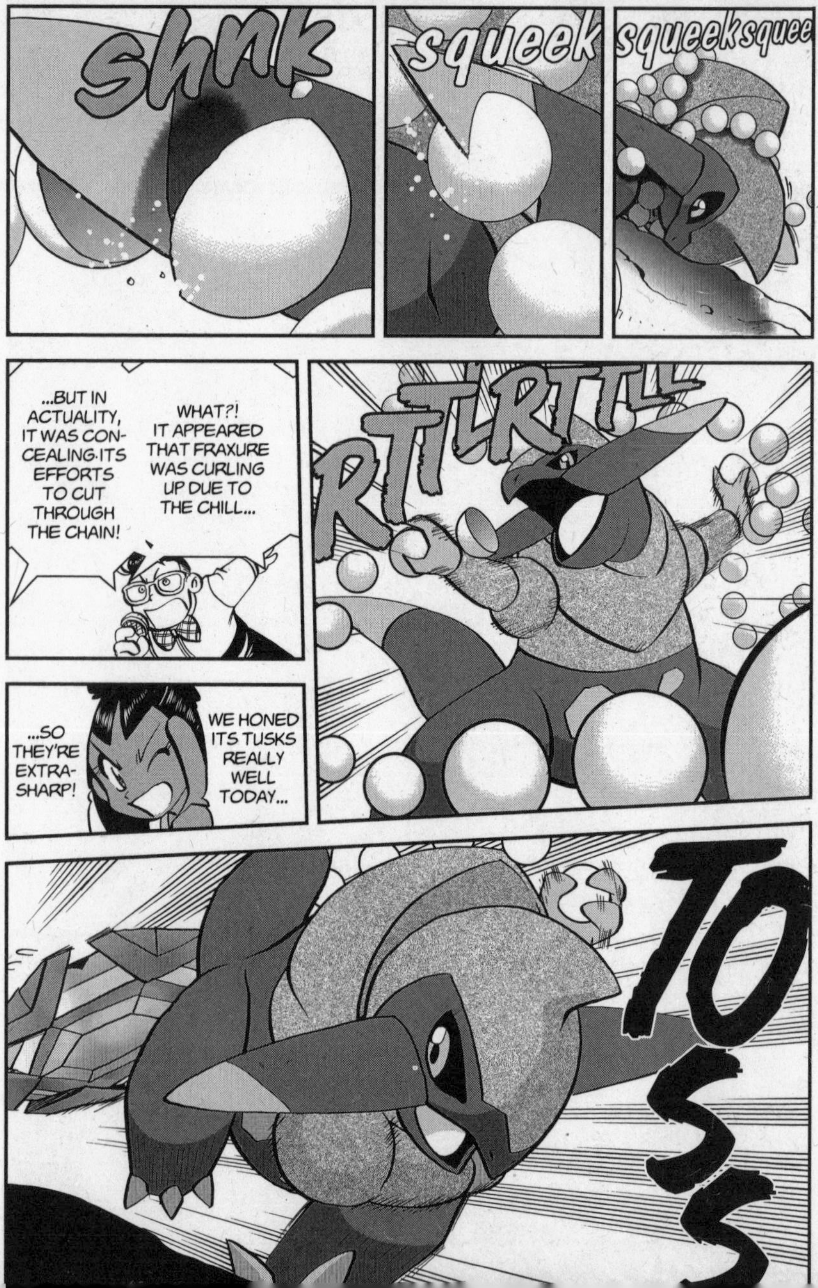
squeeksquee
squeek
shnk
RTTLRTTLL
WHAT?! IT APPEARED THAT FRAXURE WAS CURLING UP DUE TO THE CHILL...
...BUT IN ACTUALITY, IT WAS CONCEALING ITS EFFORTS TO CUT THROUGH THE CHAIN!
WE HONED ITS TUSKS REALLY WELL TODAY...
...SO THEY'RE EXTRA-SHARP!
TOSS

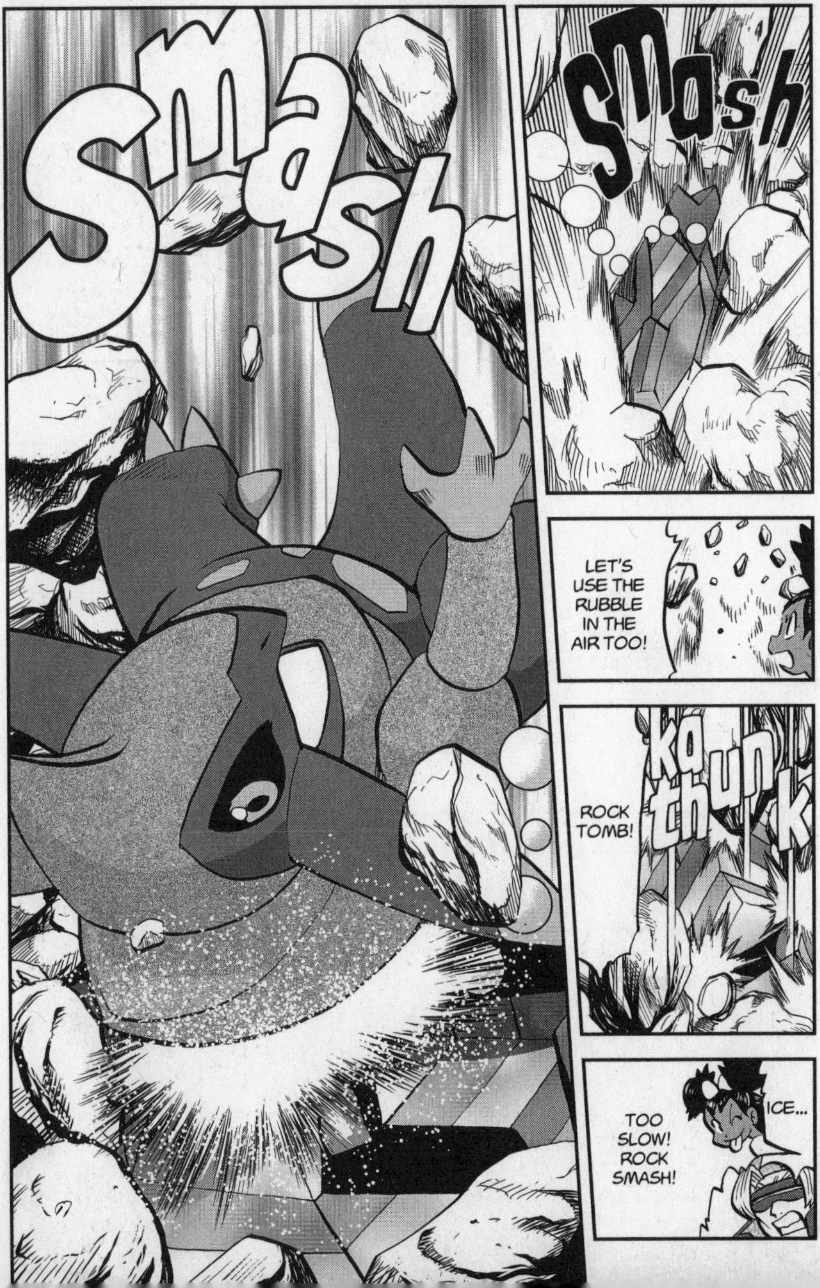
SMASH
LET'S USE THE RUBBLE IN THE AIR TOO!
ROCK TOMB!
KATHUNK
ICE...
TOO SLOW! ROCK SMASH!
SMASH

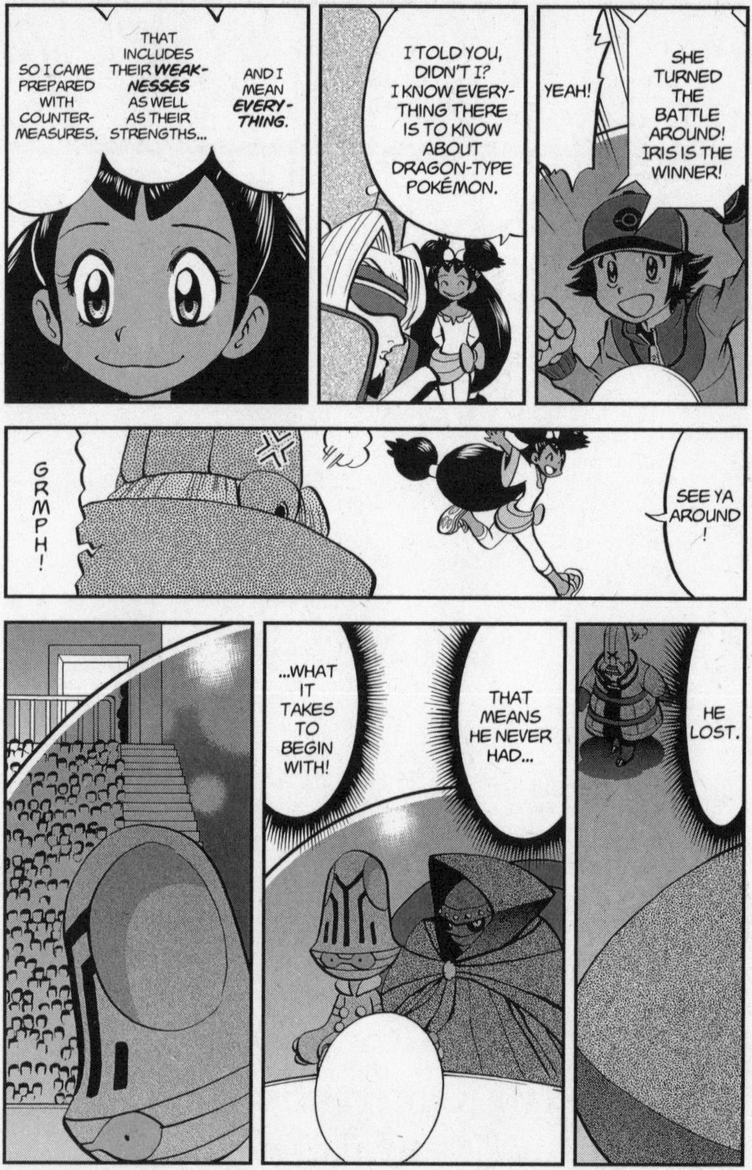
SHE TURNED THE BATTLE AROUND! IRIS IS THE WINNER!
YEAH!
I TOLD YOU, DIDN'T I? I KNOW EVERYTHING THERE IS TO KNOW ABOUT DRAGON-TYPE POKÉMON.
AND I MEAN **EVERYTHING**.
THAT INCLUDES THEIR **WEAKNESSES** AS WELL AS THEIR STRENGTHS...
SO I CAME PREPARED WITH COUNTERMEASURES.
SEE YA AROUND!
GRMPH!
HE LOST.
THAT MEANS HE NEVER HAD...
...WHAT IT TAKES TO BEGIN WITH!

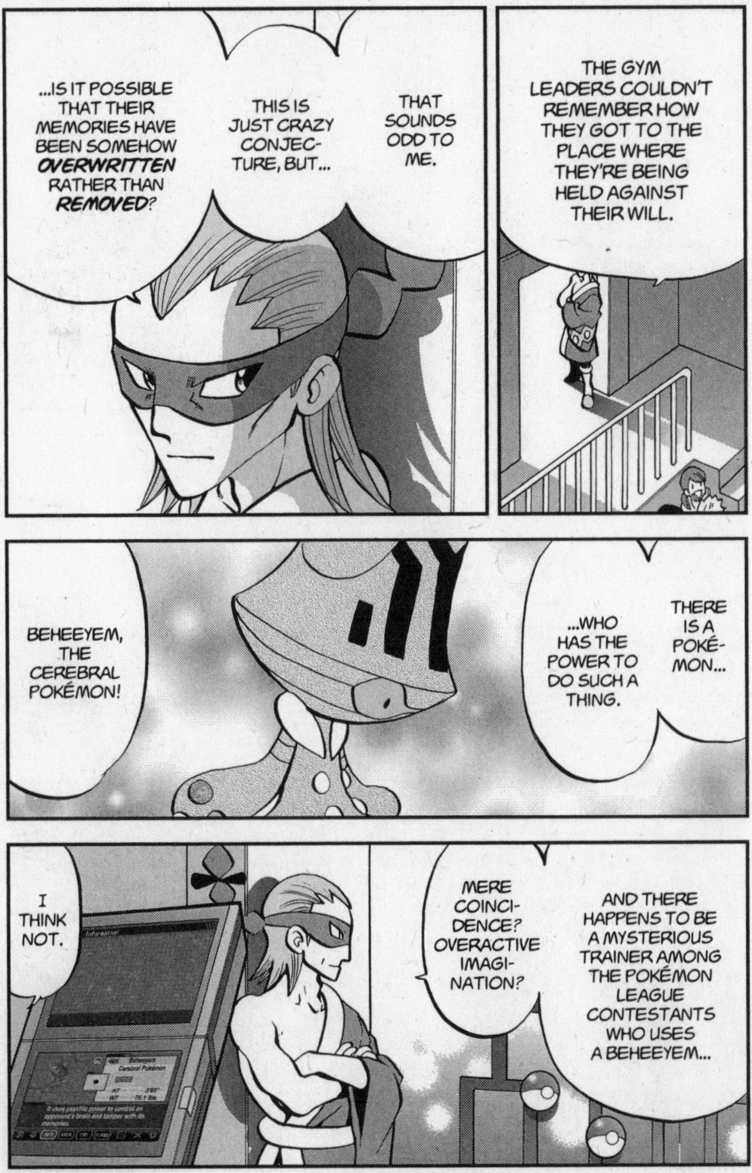
THE GYM LEADERS COULDN'T REMEMBER HOW THEY GOT TO THE PLACE WHERE THEY'RE BEING HELD AGAINST THEIR WILL.
THAT SOUNDS ODD TO ME.
THIS IS JUST CRAZY CONJECTURE, BUT...
...IS IT POSSIBLE THAT THEIR MEMORIES HAVE BEEN SOMEHOW ***OVERWRITTEN*** RATHER THAN ***REMOVED***?
THERE IS A POKÉMON...
...WHO HAS THE POWER TO DO SUCH A THING.
BEHEEYEM, THE CEREBRAL POKÉMON!
AND THERE HAPPENS TO BE A MYSTERIOUS TRAINER AMONG THE POKÉMON LEAGUE CONTESTANTS WHO USES A BEHEEYEM...
MERE COINCIDENCE? OVERACTIVE IMAGINATION?
I THINK NOT.
Information
Beheeyem
Cerebral Pokémon
It uses psychic power to control an opponent's brain and tamper with its memories.

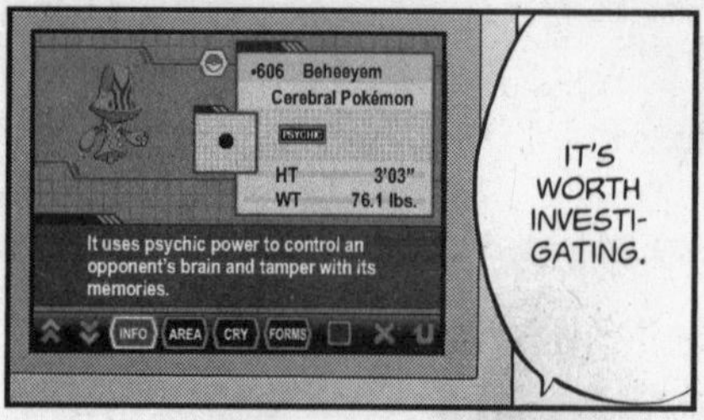
•606 Beheeyem
Cerebral Pokémon
PSYCHIC
HT 3'03"
WT 76.1 lbs.
It uses psychic power to control an opponent's brain and tamper with its memories.
INFO AREA CRY FORMS
IT'S WORTH INVESTI-GATING.

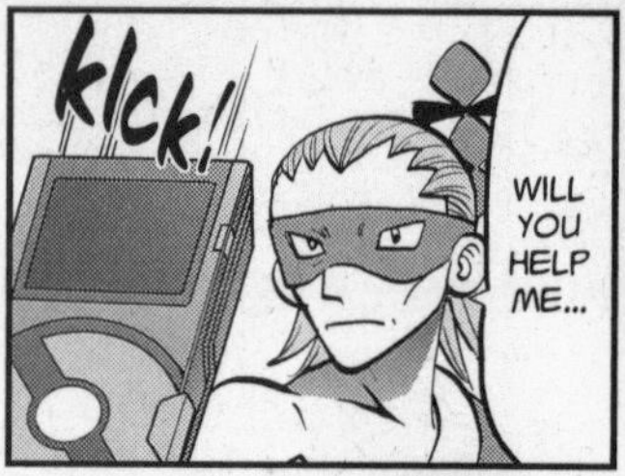
klck!
WILL YOU HELP ME...

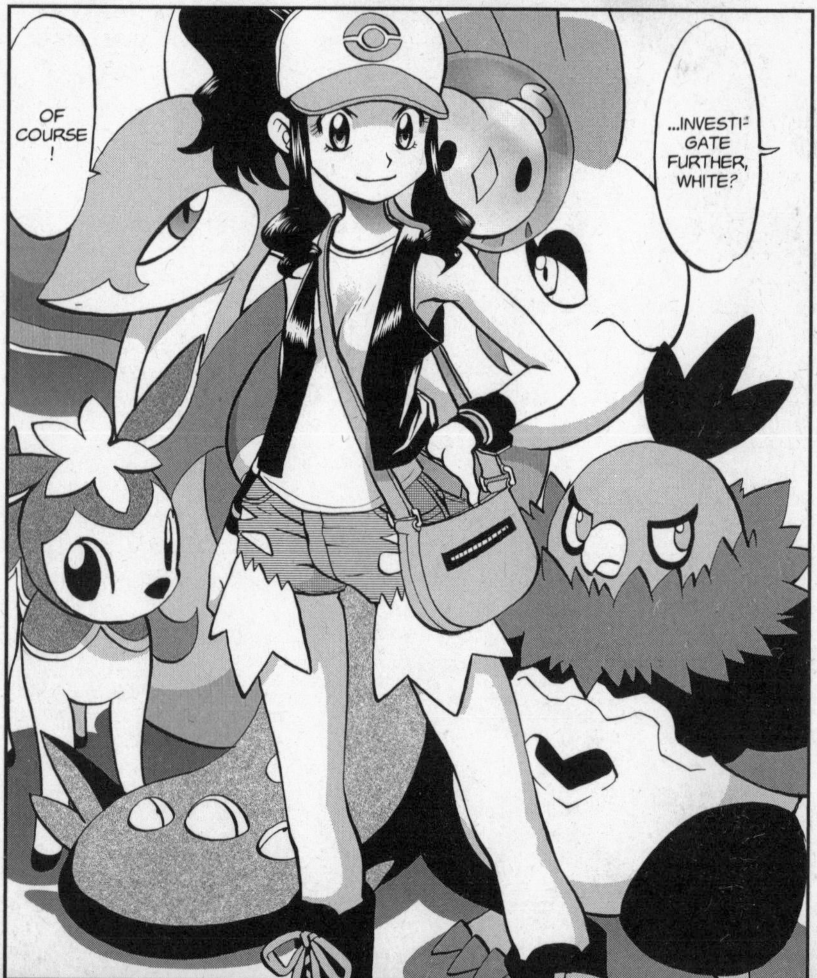
...INVESTI-GATE FURTHER, WHITE?
OF COURSE!

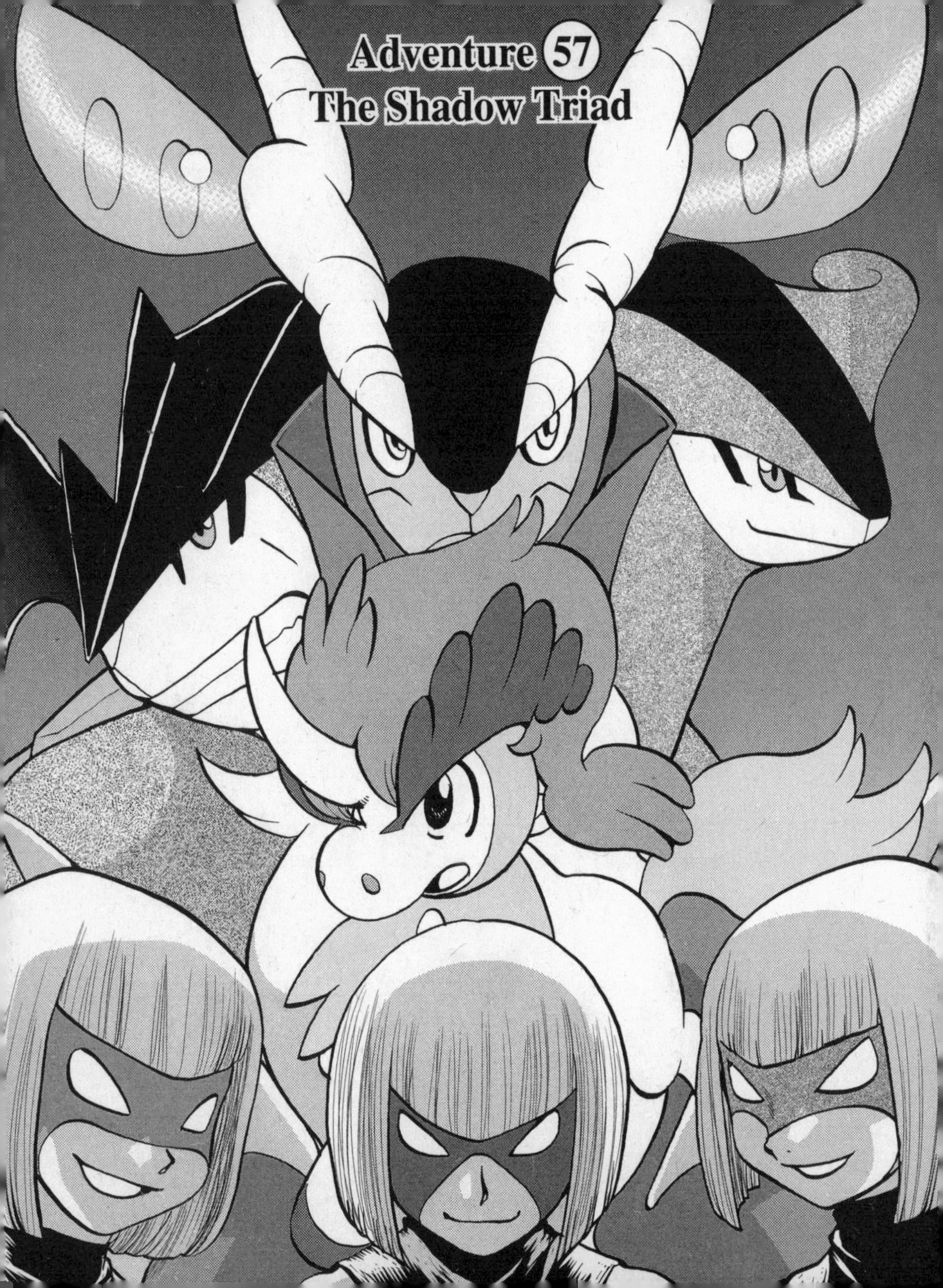
Adventure 57
The Shadow Triad

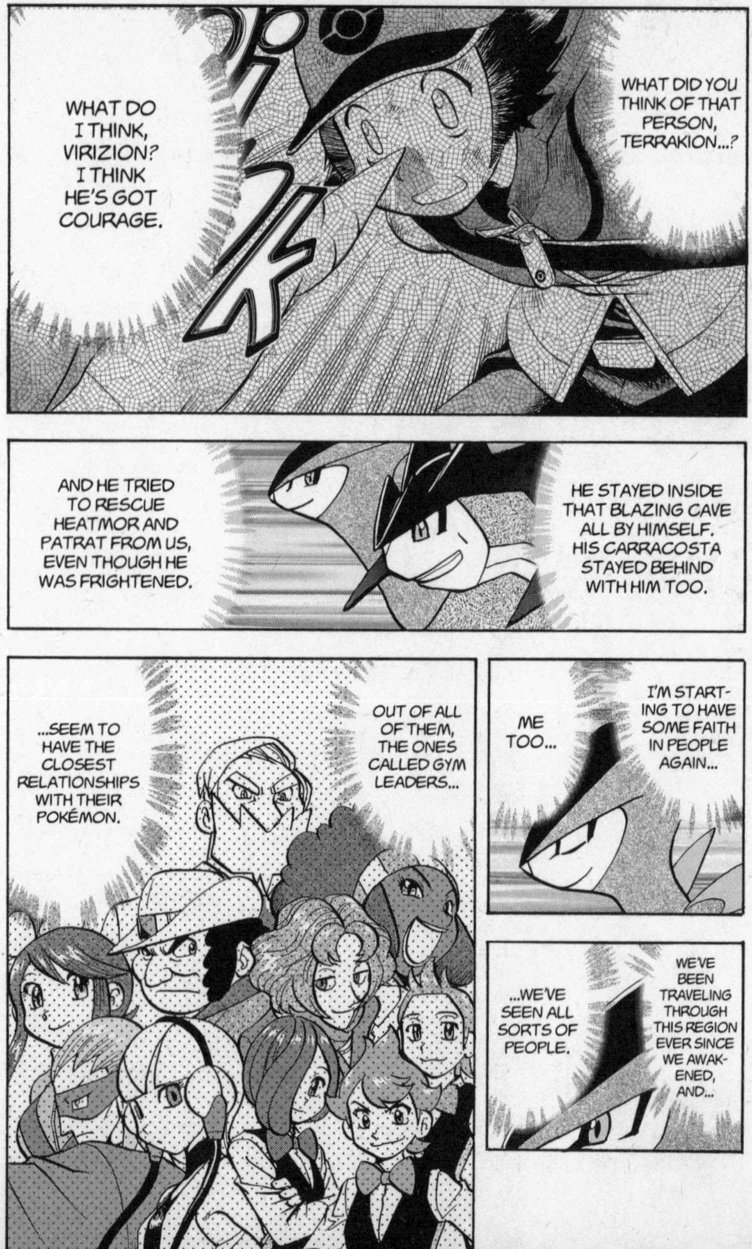
WHAT DID YOU THINK OF THAT PERSON, TERRAKION...?
WHAT DO I THINK, VIRIZION? I THINK HE'S GOT COURAGE.
HE STAYED INSIDE THAT BLAZING CAVE ALL BY HIMSELF. HIS CARRACOSTA STAYED BEHIND WITH HIM TOO.
AND HE TRIED TO RESCUE HEATMOR AND PATRAT FROM US, EVEN THOUGH HE WAS FRIGHTENED.
I'M STARTING TO HAVE SOME FAITH IN PEOPLE AGAIN...
ME TOO...
WE'VE BEEN TRAVELING THROUGH THIS REGION EVER SINCE WE AWAKENED, AND...
...WE'VE SEEN ALL SORTS OF PEOPLE.
OUT OF ALL OF THEM, THE ONES CALLED GYM LEADERS...
...SEEM TO HAVE THE CLOSEST RELATIONSHIPS WITH THEIR POKÉMON.

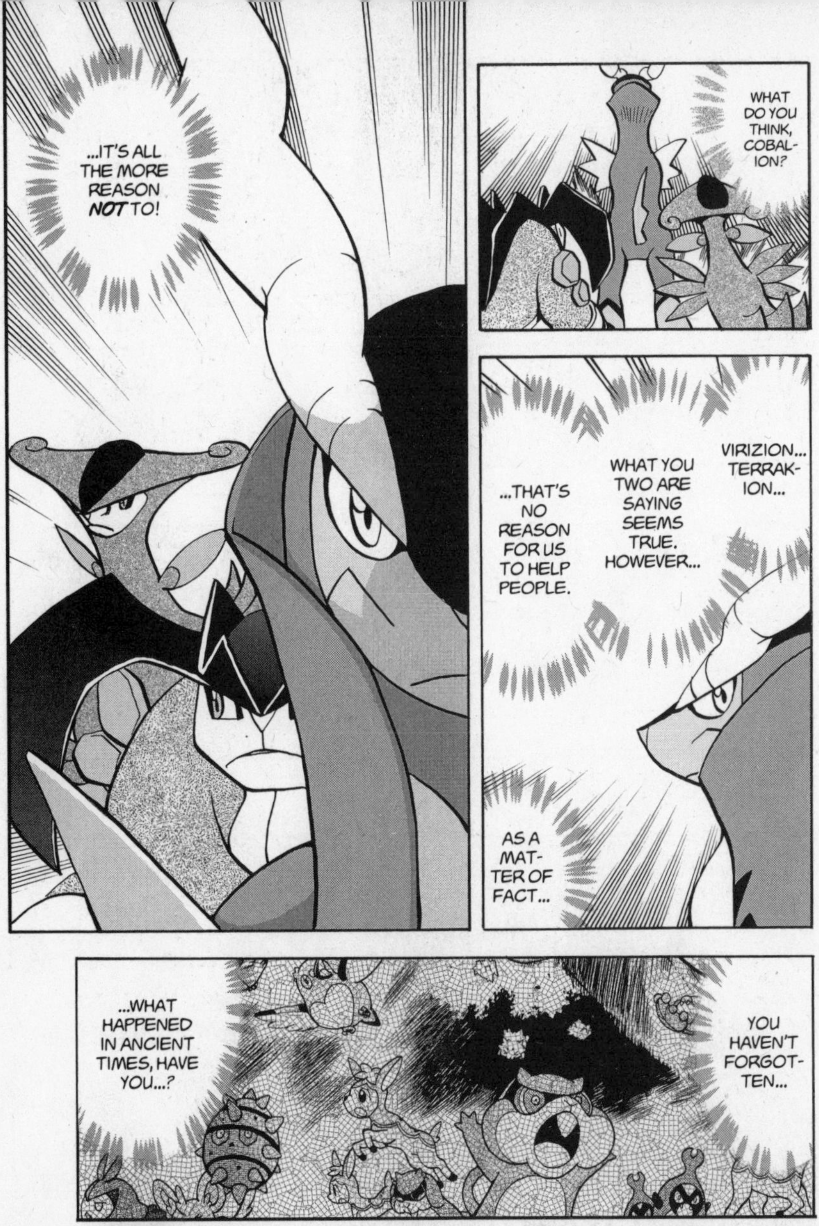
WHAT DO YOU THINK, COBAL-ION?
VIRIZION... TERRAK-ION...
WHAT YOU TWO ARE SAYING SEEMS TRUE. HOWEVER...
...THAT'S NO REASON FOR US TO HELP PEOPLE.
AS A MAT-TER OF FACT...
...IT'S ALL THE MORE REASON NOT TO!
YOU HAVEN'T FORGOT-TEN...
...WHAT HAPPENED IN ANCIENT TIMES, HAVE YOU...?

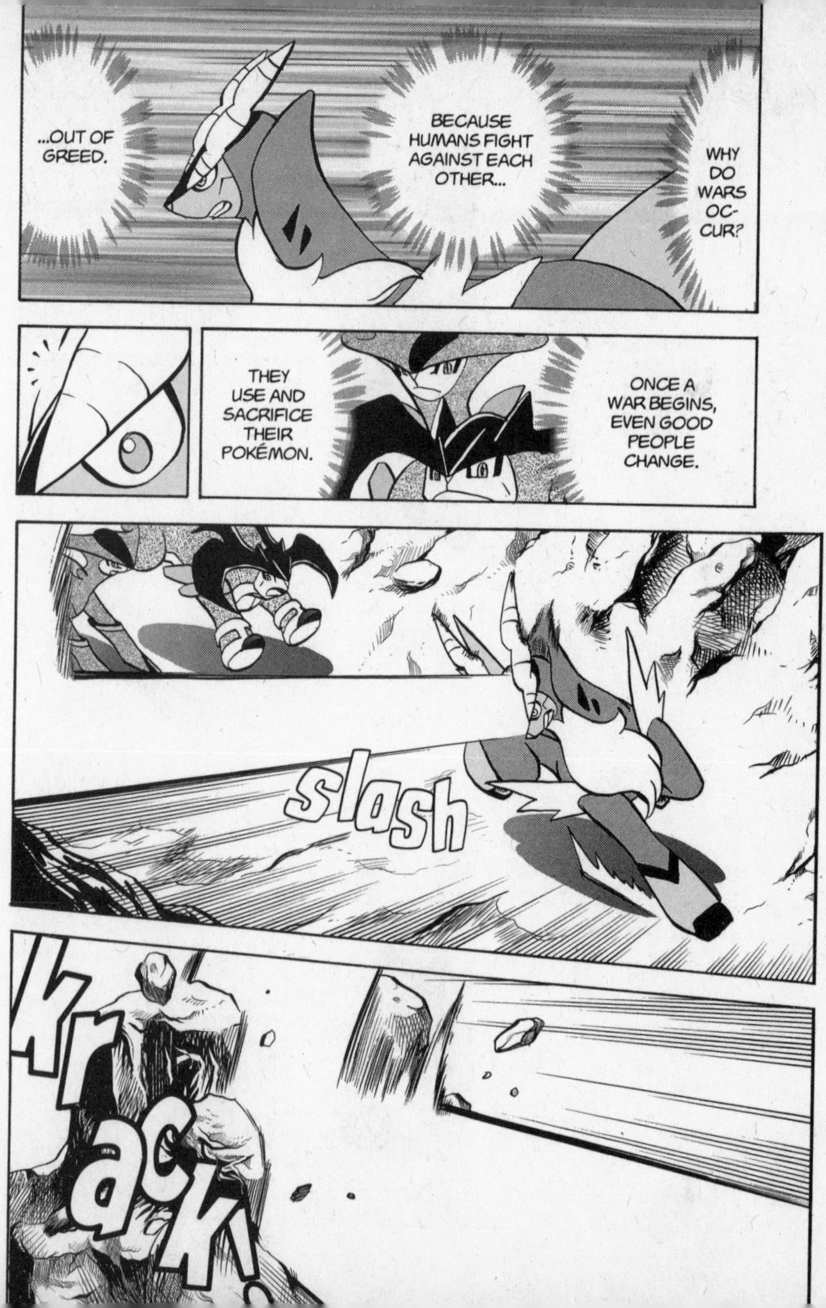
WHY DO WARS OC-CUR?
BECAUSE HUMANS FIGHT AGAINST EACH OTHER...
...OUT OF GREED.
ONCE A WAR BEGINS, EVEN GOOD PEOPLE CHANGE.
THEY USE AND SACRIFICE THEIR POKÉMON.
slash
krack!

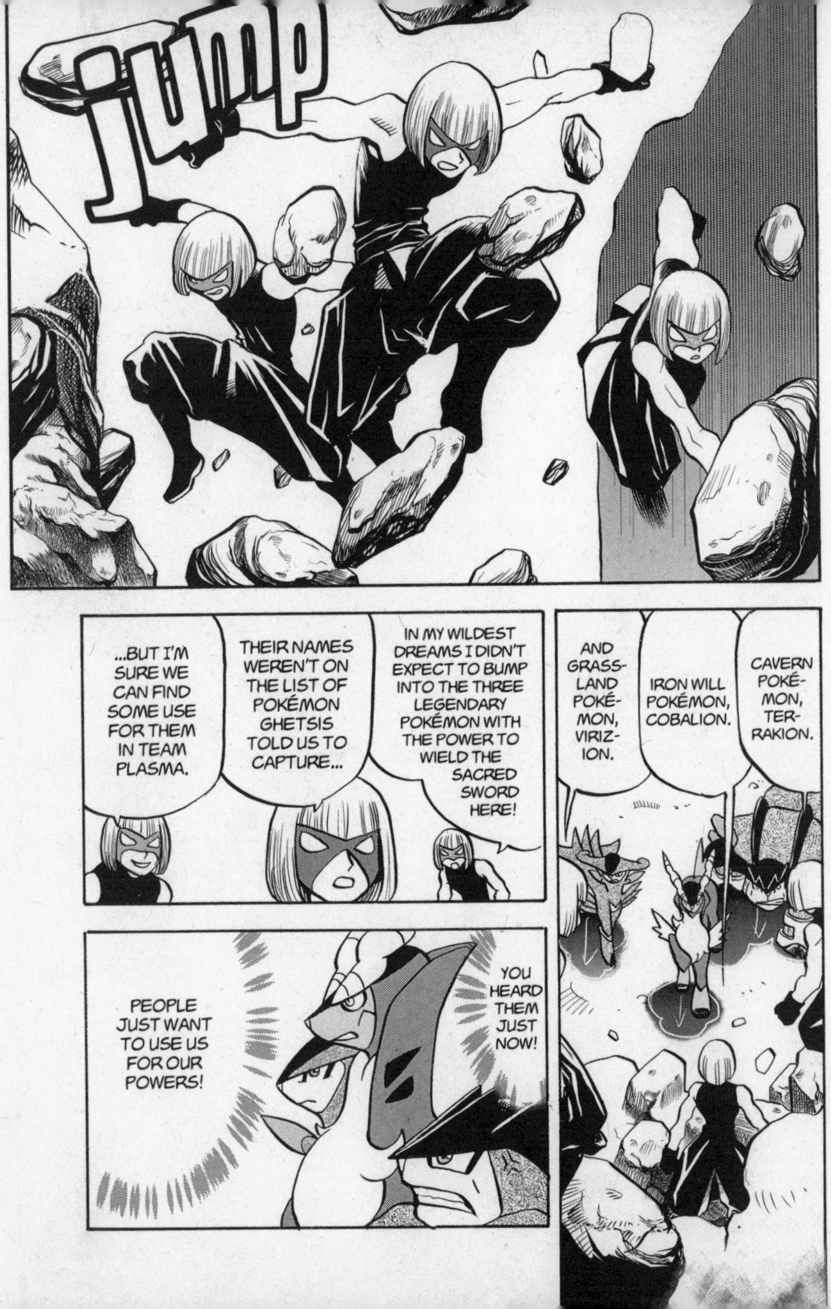
JUMP
CAVERN POKÉMON, TERRAKION.
IRON WILL POKÉMON, COBALION.
AND GRASSLAND POKÉMON, VIRIZION.
IN MY WILDEST DREAMS I DIDN'T EXPECT TO BUMP INTO THE THREE LEGENDARY POKÉMON WITH THE POWER TO WIELD THE SACRED SWORD HERE!
THEIR NAMES WEREN'T ON THE LIST OF POKÉMON GHETSIS TOLD US TO CAPTURE...
...BUT I'M SURE WE CAN FIND SOME USE FOR THEM IN TEAM PLASMA.
YOU HEARD THEM JUST NOW!
PEOPLE JUST WANT TO USE US FOR OUR POWERS!

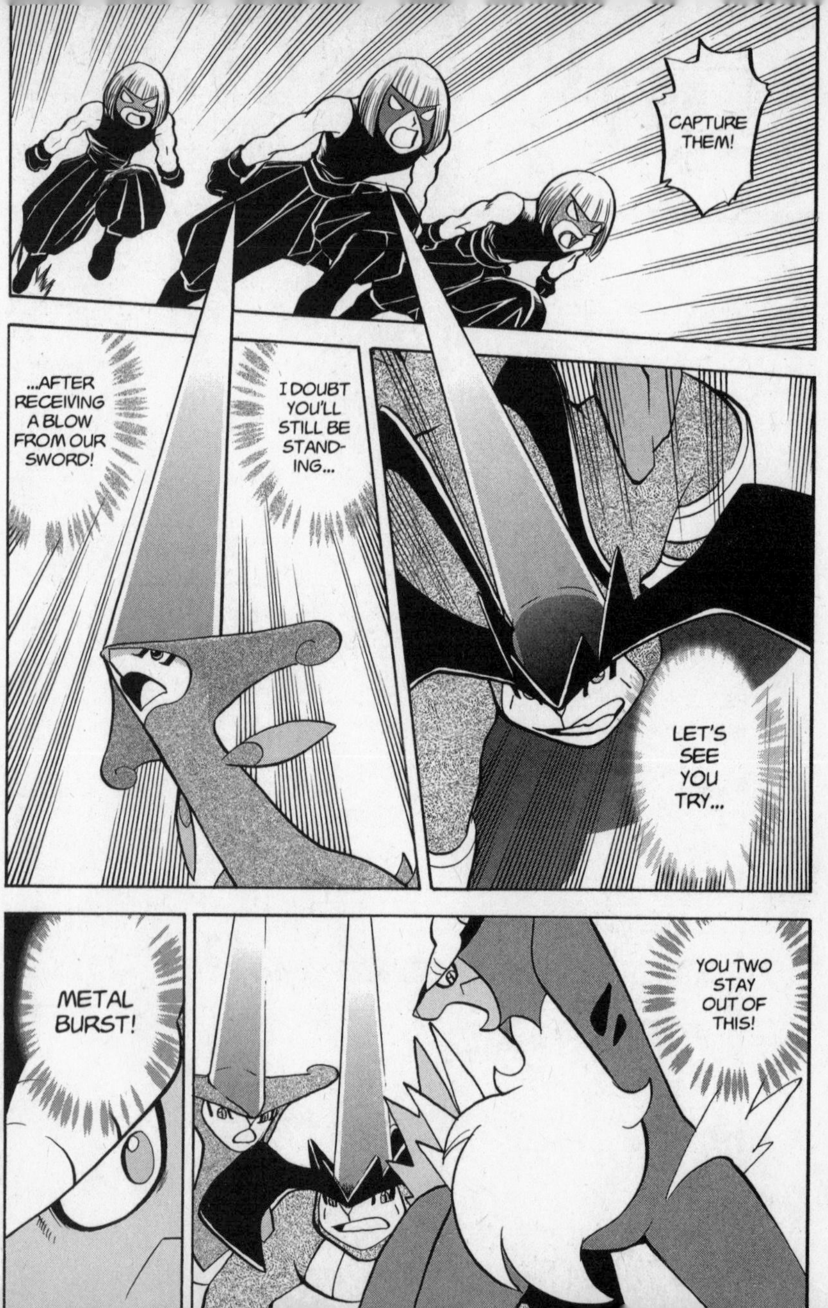
CAPTURE THEM!
LET'S SEE YOU TRY...
I DOUBT YOU'LL STILL BE STANDING...
...AFTER RECEIVING A BLOW FROM OUR SWORD!
YOU TWO STAY OUT OF THIS!
METAL BURST!

THEY DISAP-PEARED
...

FORGET ABOUT THEM. WE HAVE TO GET BACK TO WHERE WE STARTED.

...

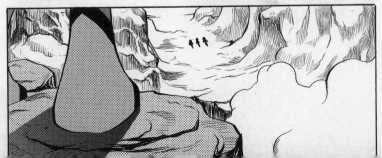

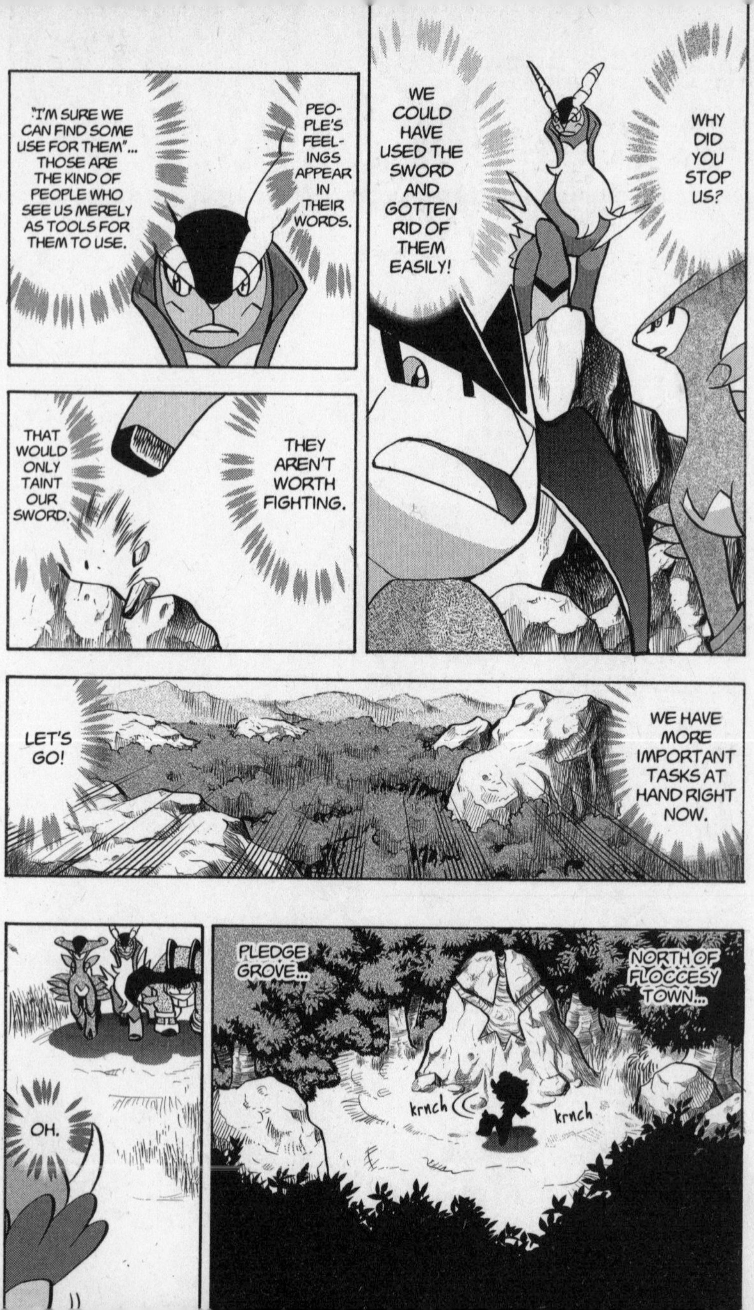
WHY DID YOU STOP US?
WE COULD HAVE USED THE SWORD AND GOTTEN RID OF THEM EASILY!
PEOPLE'S FEELINGS APPEAR IN THEIR WORDS.
"I'M SURE WE CAN FIND SOME USE FOR THEM"... THOSE ARE THE KIND OF PEOPLE WHO SEE US MERELY AS TOOLS FOR THEM TO USE.
THEY AREN'T WORTH FIGHTING.
THAT WOULD ONLY TAINT OUR SWORD.
WE HAVE MORE IMPORTANT TASKS AT HAND RIGHT NOW.
LET'S GO!
NORTH OF FLOCCESY TOWN...
PLEDGE GROVE...
krnch
krnch
OH.

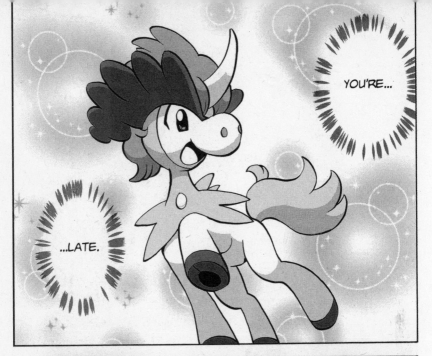

YOU'RE...
...LATE.
SORRY TO KEEP YOU WAITING.
AS OUR YOUNG APPRENTICE...
...KELDEO...
...YOU MUST MASTER THE USE OF THIS SWORD MOVE TO JOIN US.
THIS WILL BE YOUR FINAL TEST.
HAVE YOU BEEN PRACTICING EVERYTHING WE'VE TAUGHT YOU UP TILL NOW?
YES.

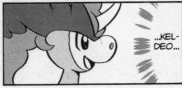

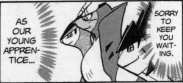

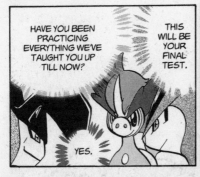

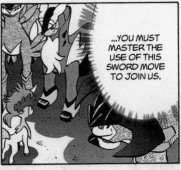

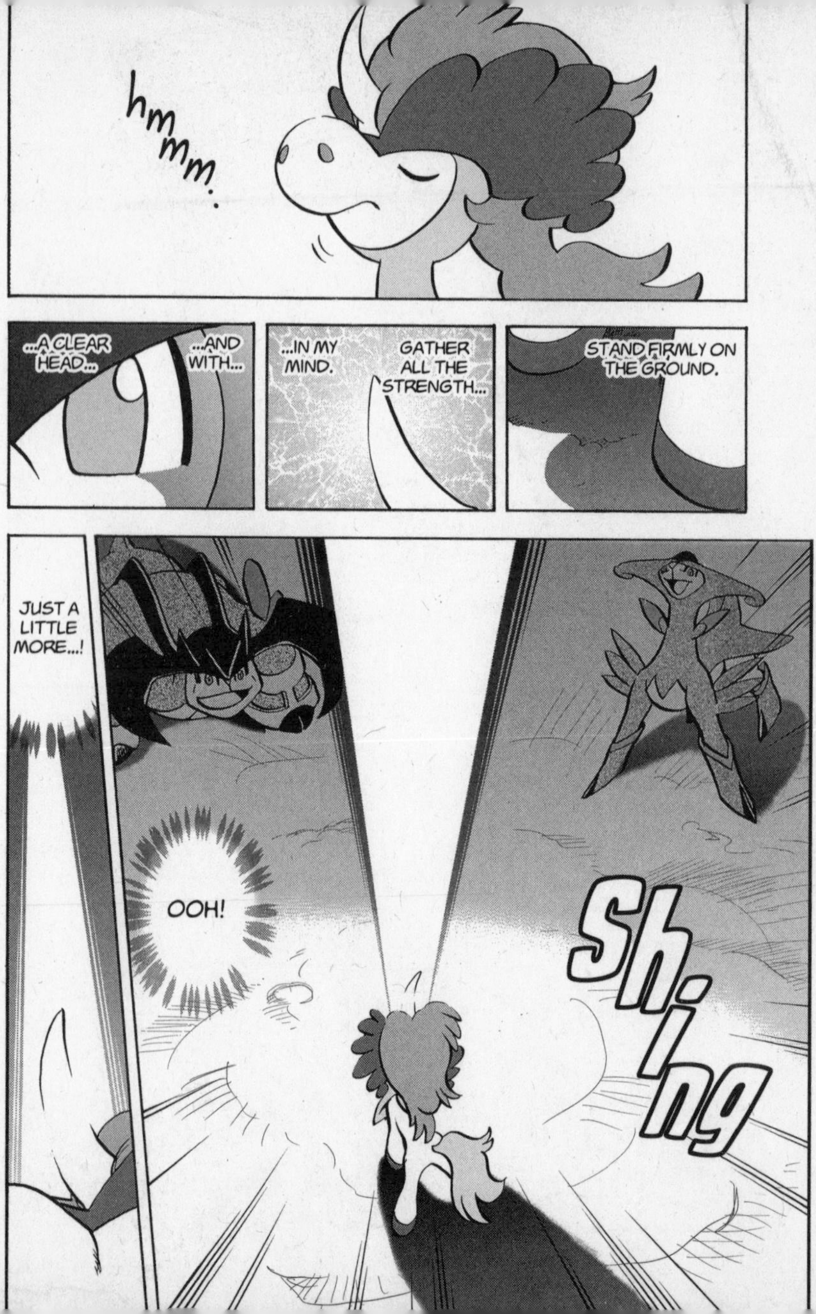
hmmm.
STAND FIRMLY ON THE GROUND.
GATHER ALL THE STRENGTH...
...IN MY MIND.
...AND WITH...
...A CLEAR HEAD...
JUST A LITTLE MORE...!
Shing
OOH!

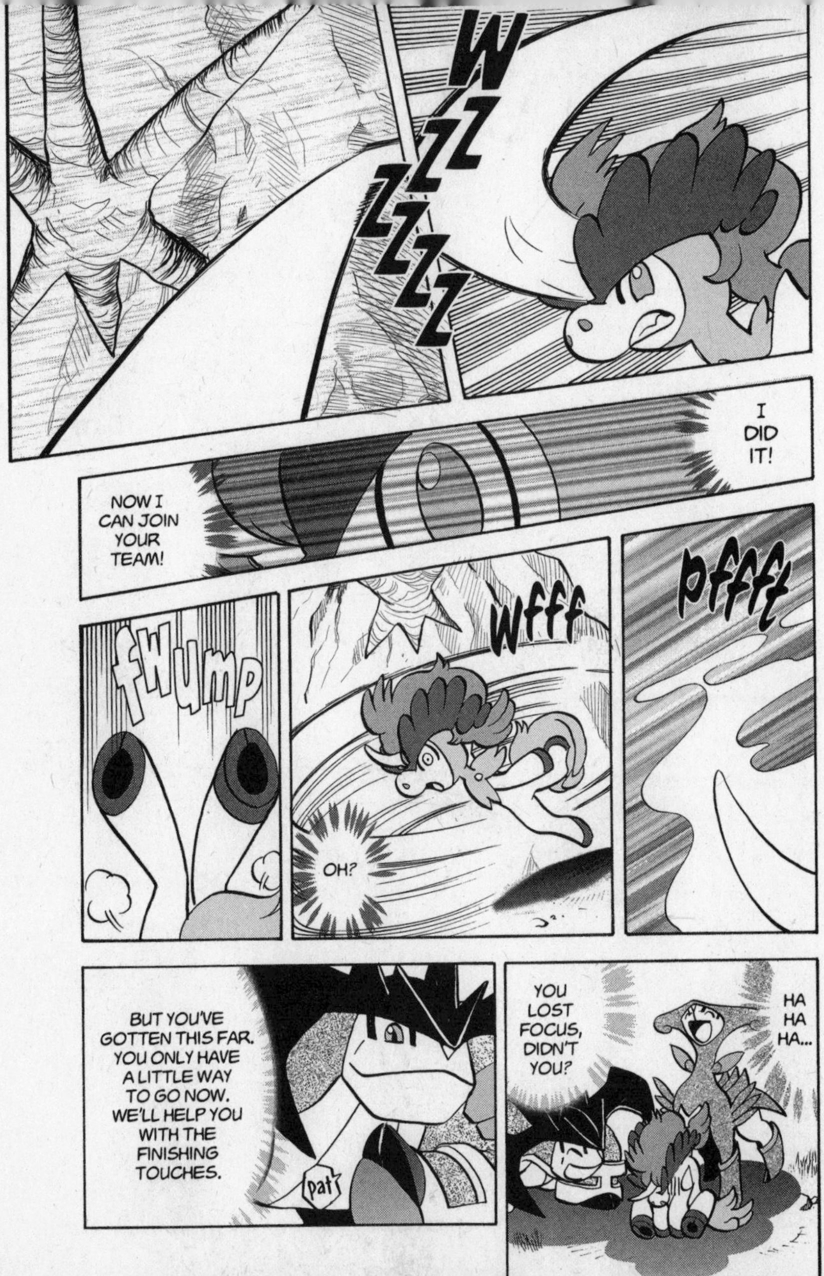
WZZZZZZ
I DID IT!
NOW I CAN JOIN YOUR TEAM!
pffft
wfff
OH?
fwump
HA HA HA...
YOU LOST FOCUS, DIDN'T YOU?
BUT YOU'VE GOTTEN THIS FAR. YOU ONLY HAVE A LITTLE WAY TO GO NOW. WE'LL HELP YOU WITH THE FINISHING TOUCHES.
pat

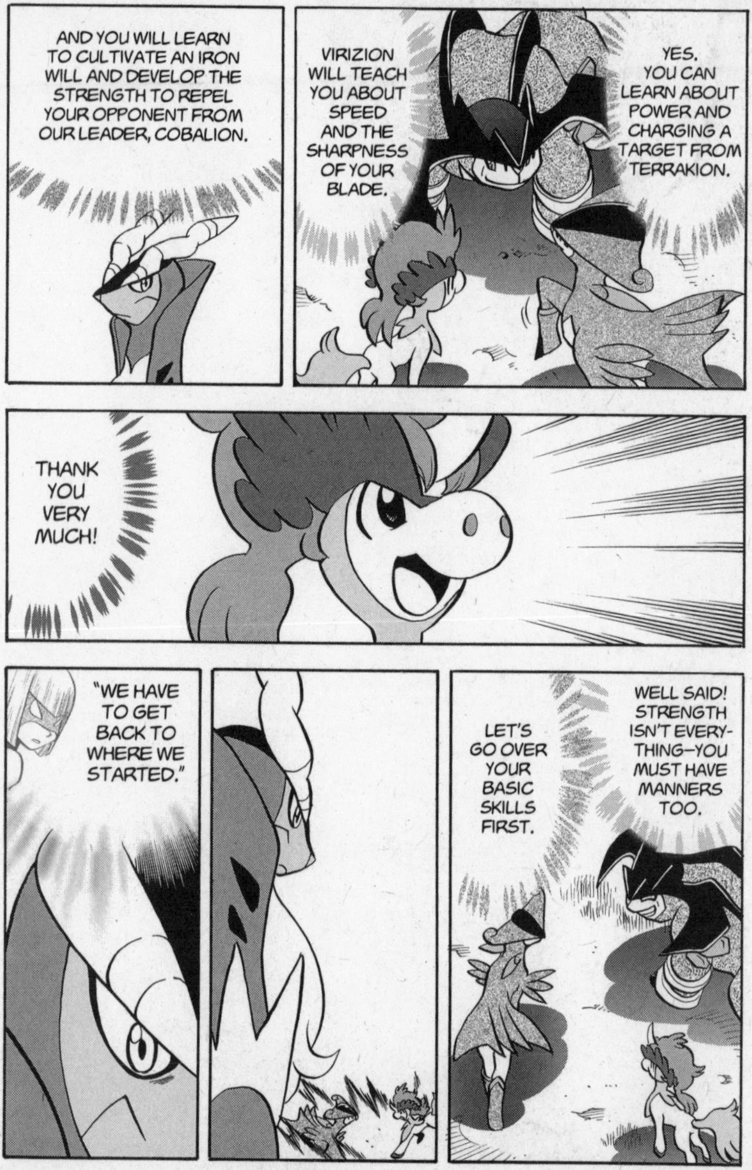
YES. YOU CAN LEARN ABOUT POWER AND CHARGING A TARGET FROM TERRAKION.
VIRIZION WILL TEACH YOU ABOUT SPEED AND THE SHARPNESS OF YOUR BLADE.
AND YOU WILL LEARN TO CULTIVATE AN IRON WILL AND DEVELOP THE STRENGTH TO REPEL YOUR OPPONENT FROM OUR LEADER, COBALION.
THANK YOU VERY MUCH!
WELL SAID! STRENGTH ISN'T EVERY-THING—YOU MUST HAVE MANNERS TOO.
LET'S GO OVER YOUR BASIC SKILLS FIRST.
"WE HAVE TO GET BACK TO WHERE WE STARTED."

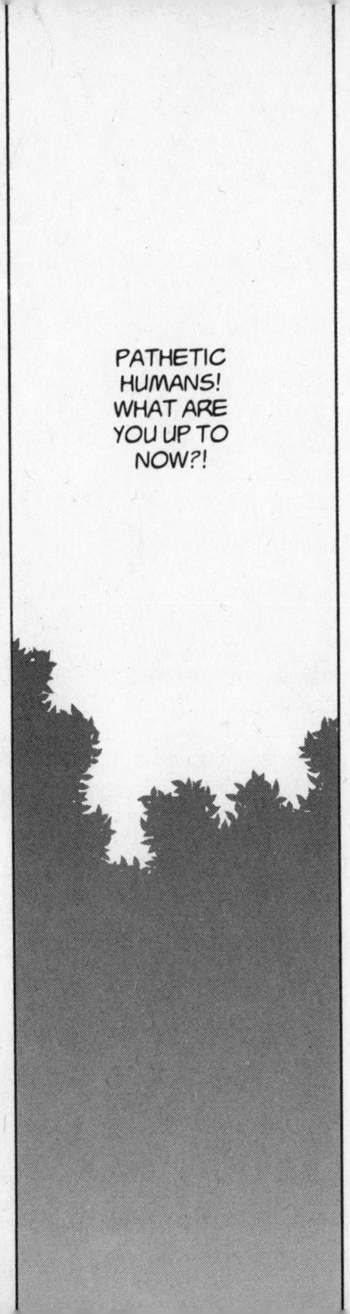
PATHETIC HUMANS! WHAT ARE YOU UP TO NOW?!

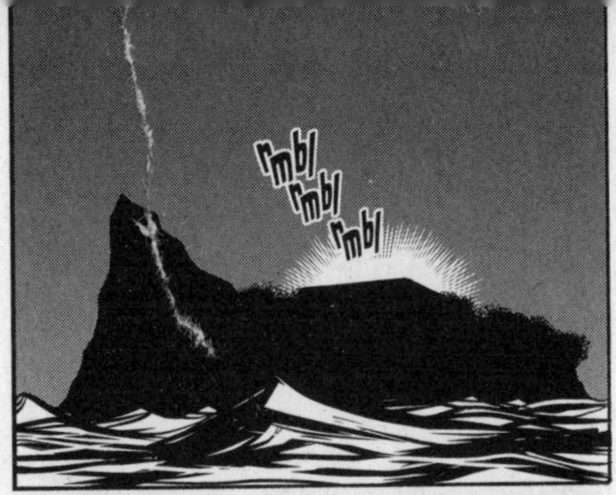
rmbl
rmbl
rmbl

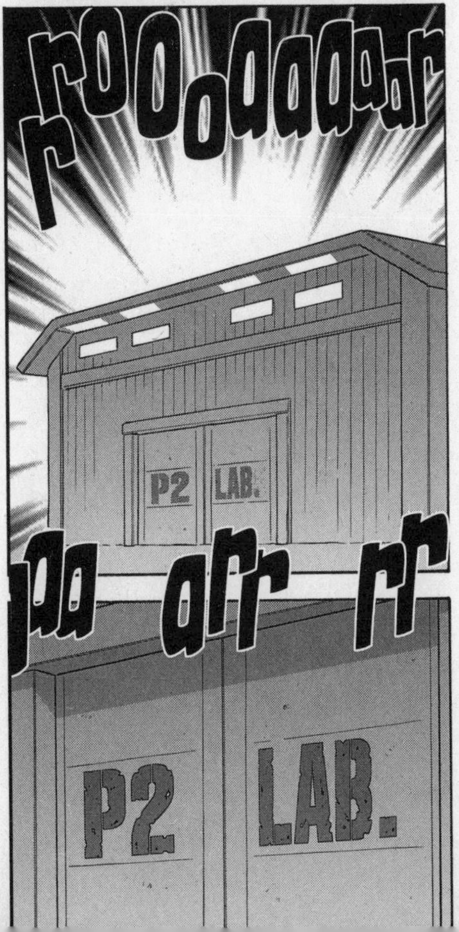
rrOOoaaaaar
P2 LAB.
P2 LAB.

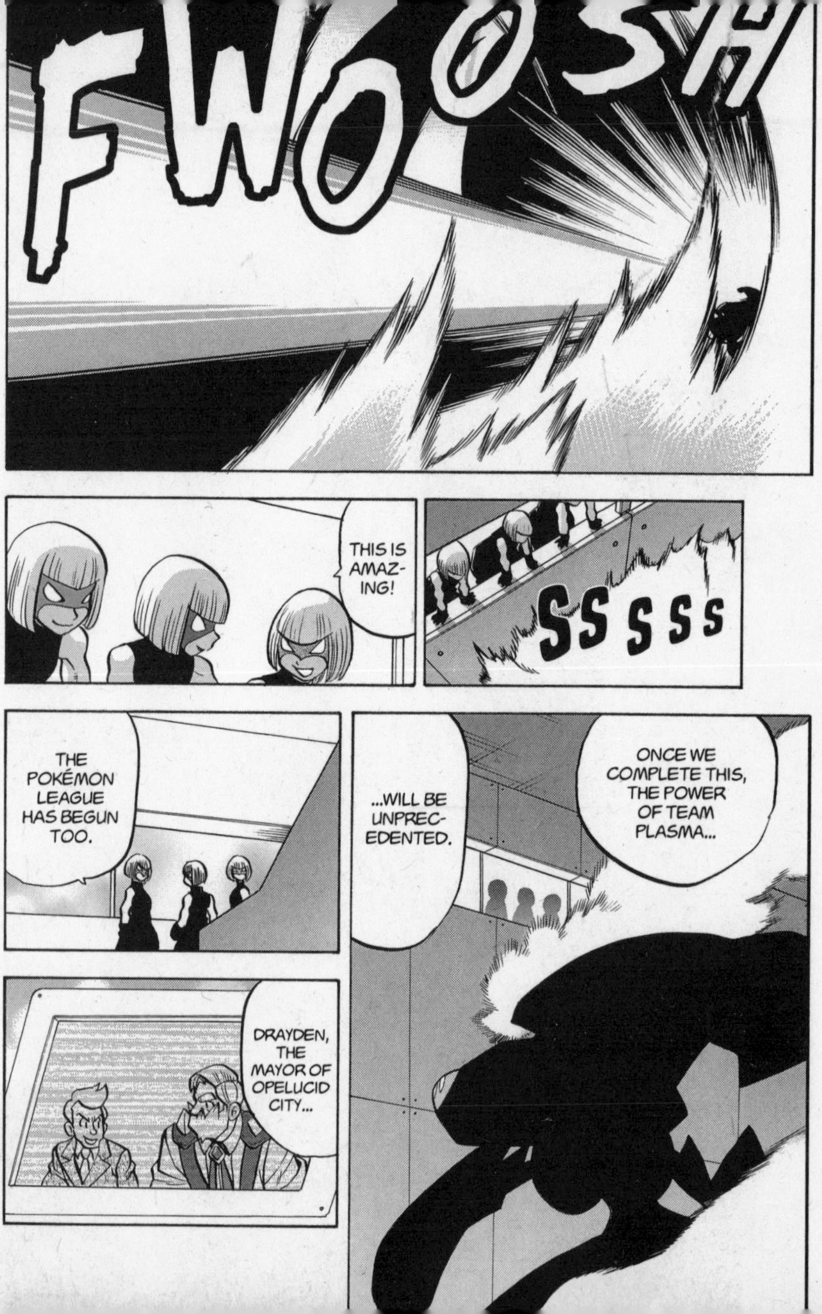
FWOOSH
SSSSS
THIS IS AMAZING!
ONCE WE COMPLETE THIS, THE POWER OF TEAM PLASMA...
...WILL BE UNPRECEDENTED.
THE POKÉMON LEAGUE HAS BEGUN TOO.
DRAYDEN, THE MAYOR OF OPELUCID CITY...

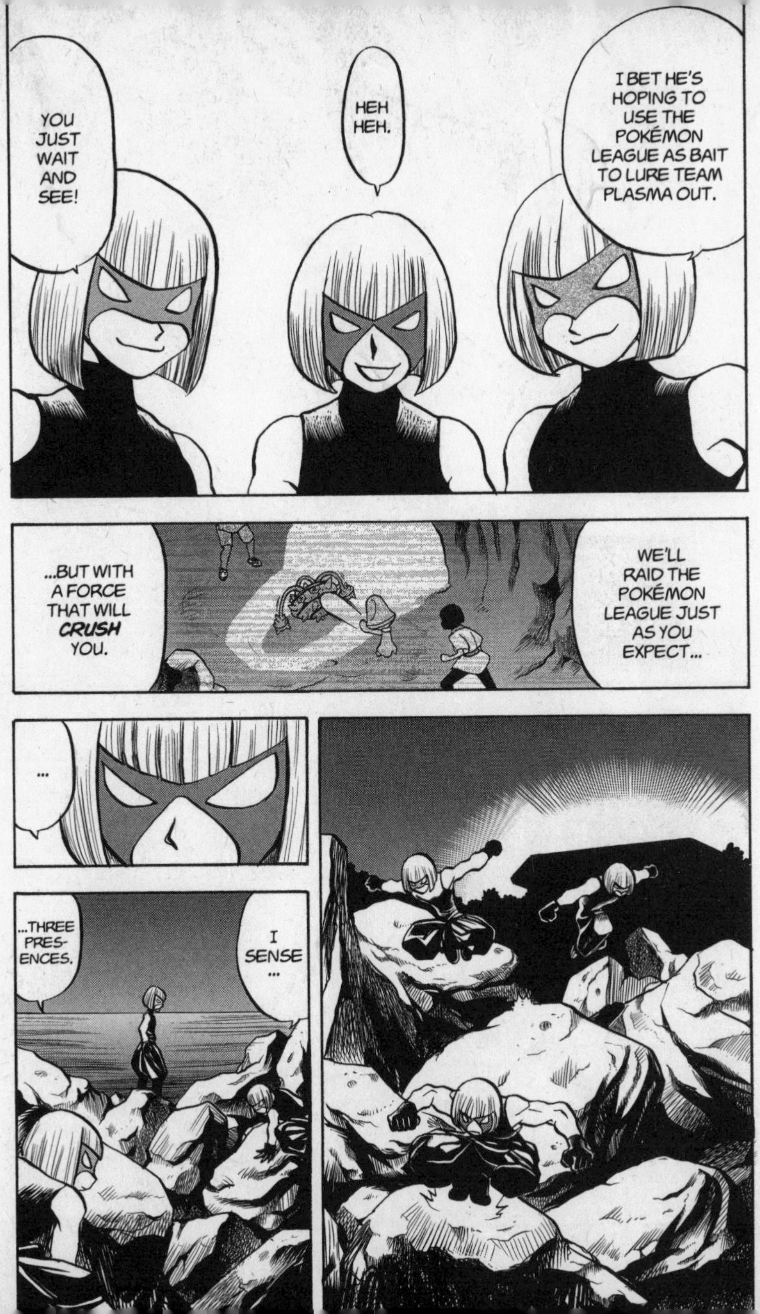

I BET HE'S HOPING TO USE THE POKÉMON LEAGUE AS BAIT TO LURE TEAM PLASMA OUT.
HEH HEH.
YOU JUST WAIT AND SEE!
WE'LL RAID THE POKÉMON LEAGUE JUST AS YOU EXPECT...
...BUT WITH A FORCE THAT WILL **CRUSH** YOU.
...
I SENSE ...
...THREE PRESENCES.

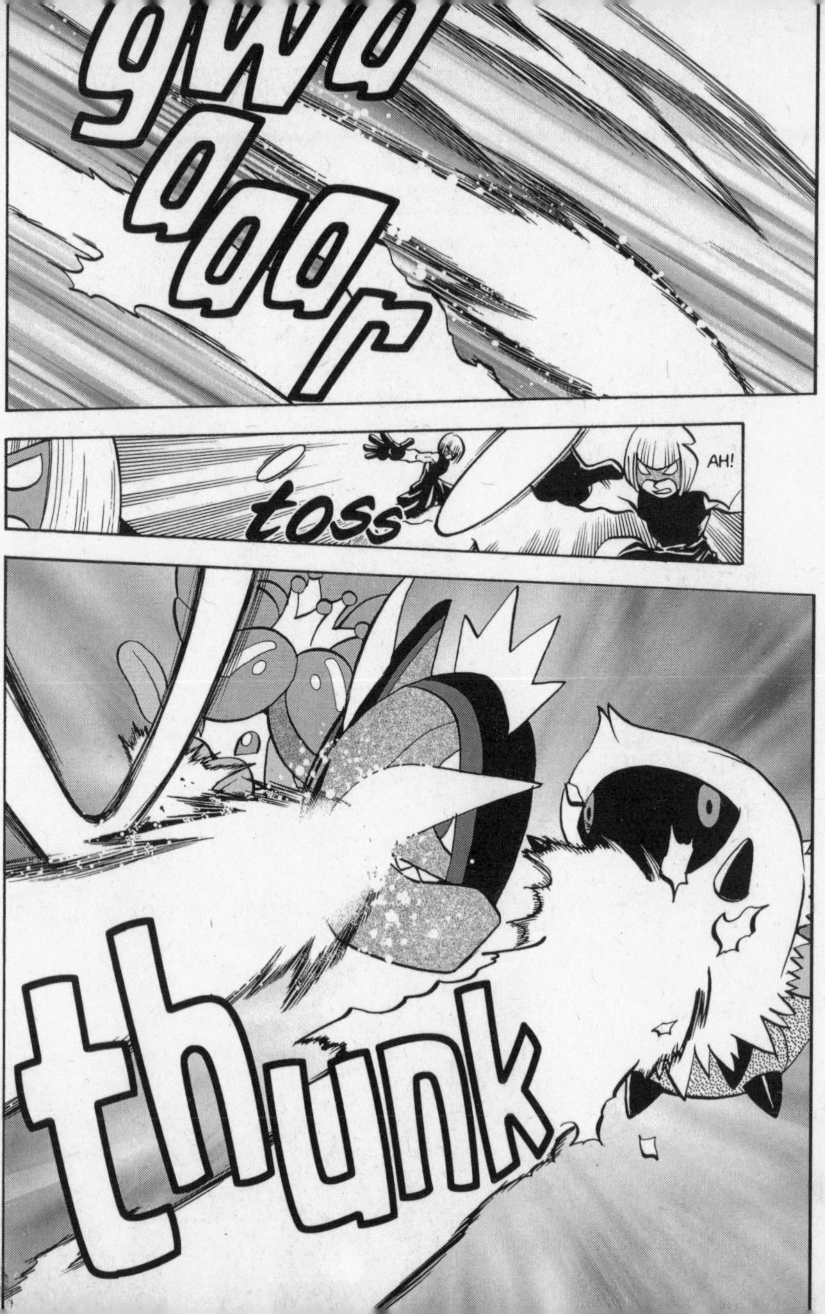
gwoaaar
AH!
toss
thunk

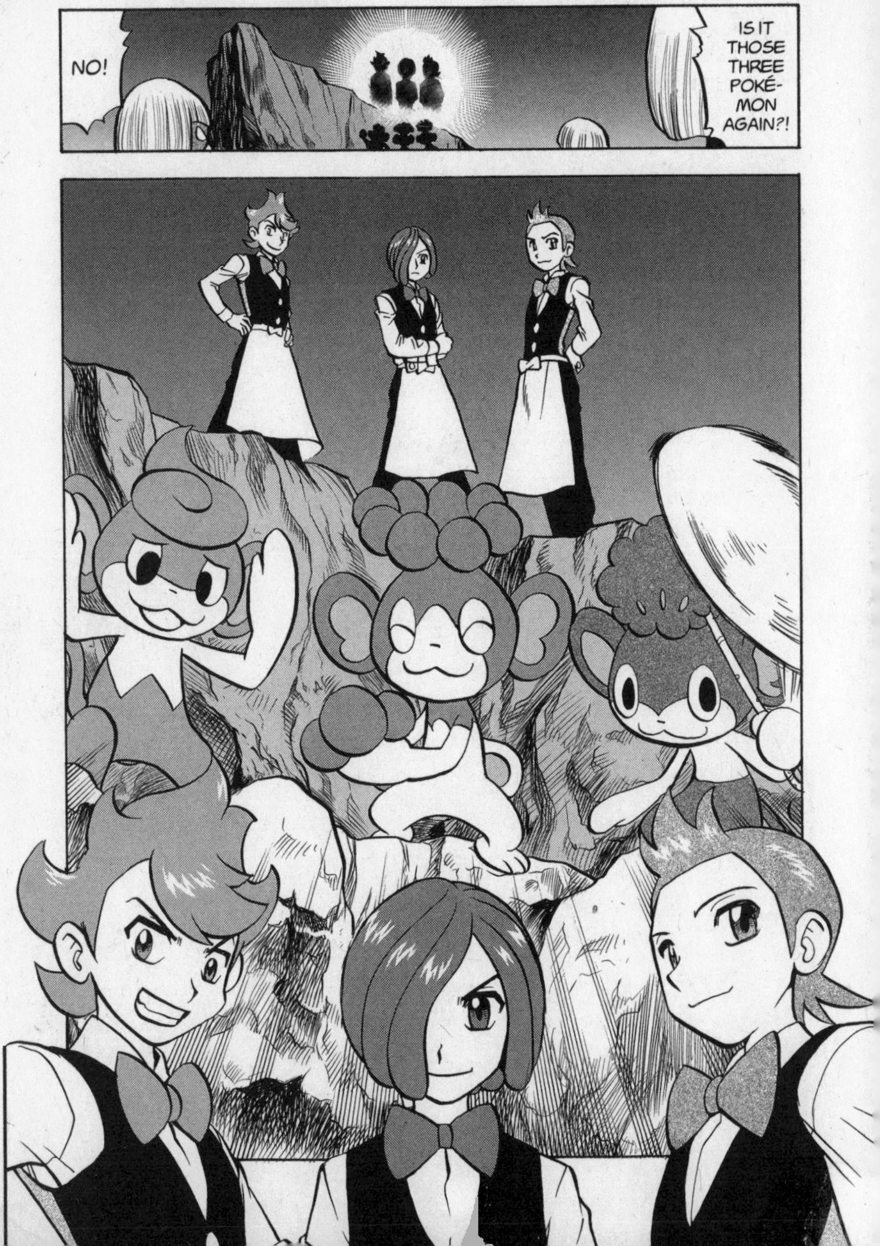
IS IT THOSE THREE POKÉ-MON AGAIN?!
NO!

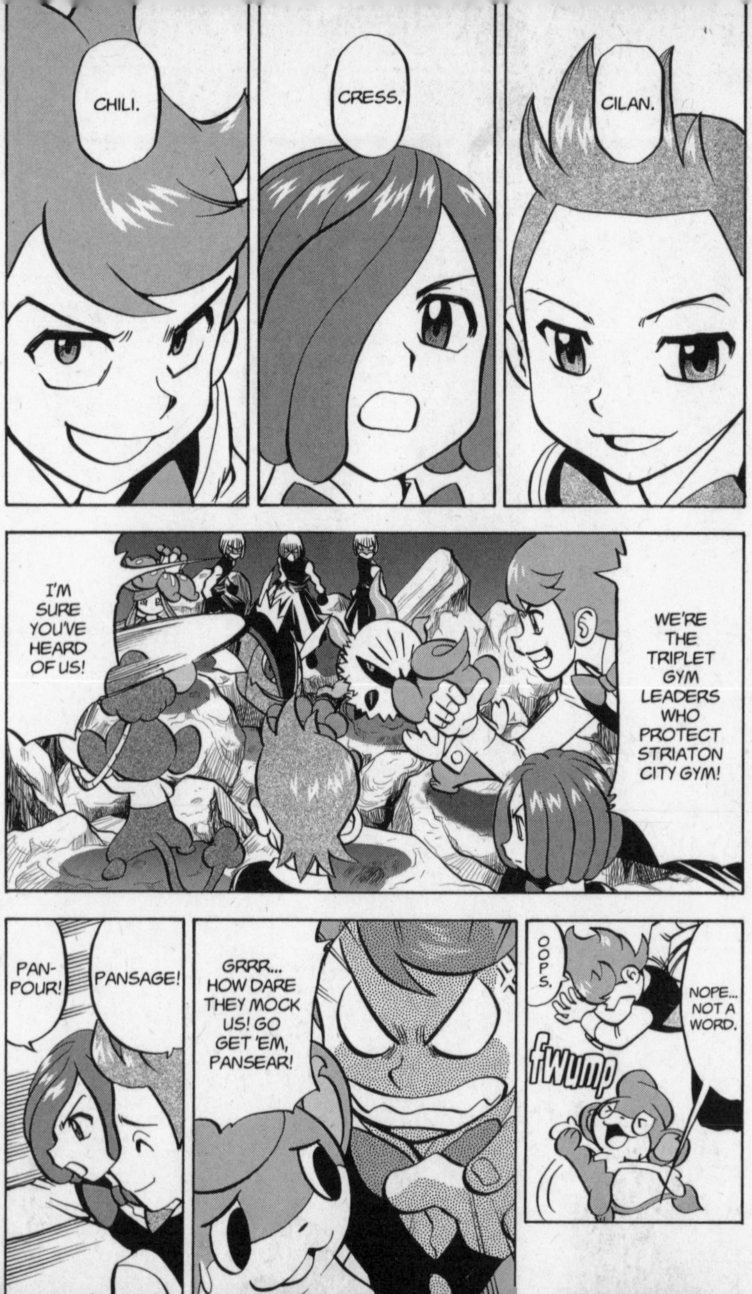
CILAN.
CRESS.
CHILI.
WE'RE THE TRIPLET GYM LEADERS WHO PROTECT STRIATON CITY GYM!
I'M SURE YOU'VE HEARD OF US!
OOPS.
NOPE... NOT A WORD.
fwump
GRRR... HOW DARE THEY MOCK US! GO GET 'EM, PANSEAR!
PANSAGE!
PAN-POUR!

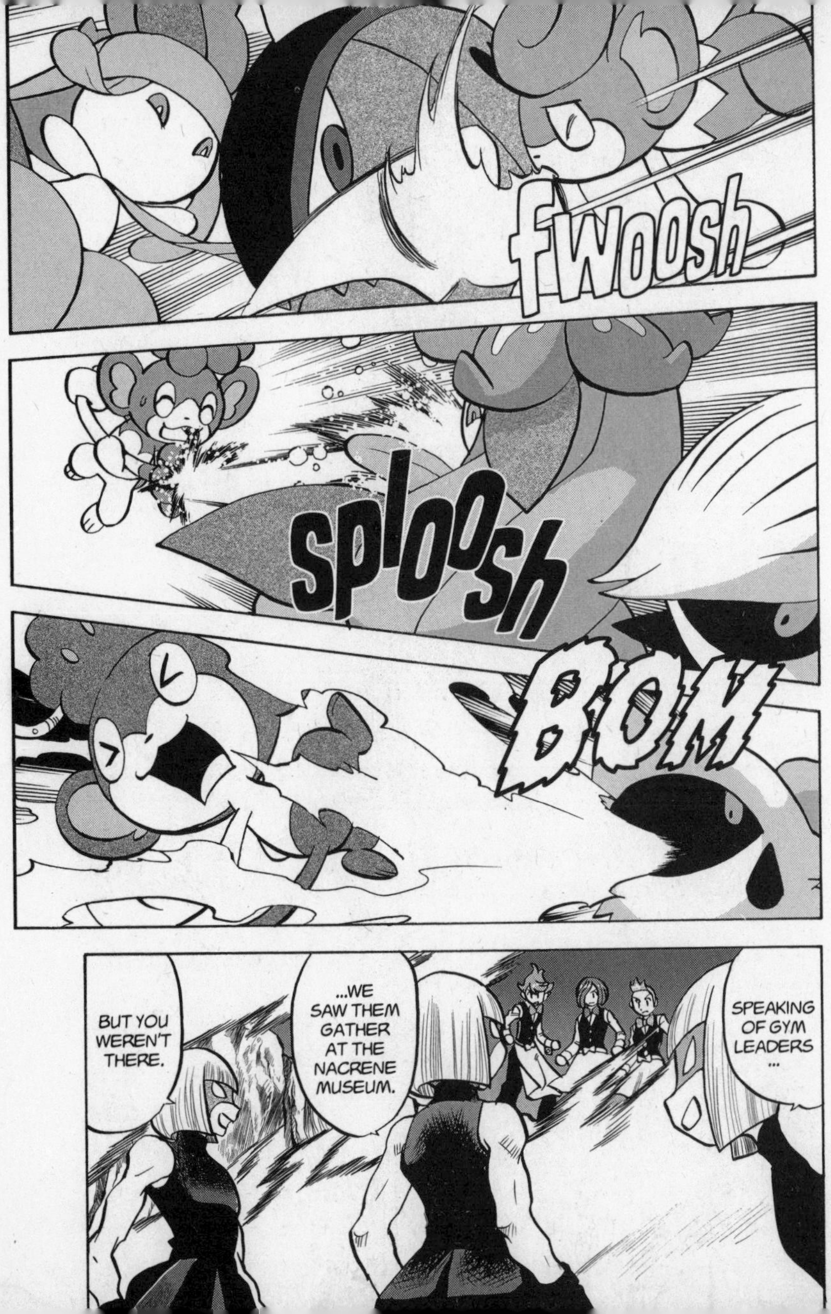
fwoosh
sploosh
BOM
SPEAKING OF GYM LEADERS ...
...WE SAW THEM GATHER AT THE NACRENE MUSEUM.
BUT YOU WEREN'T THERE.

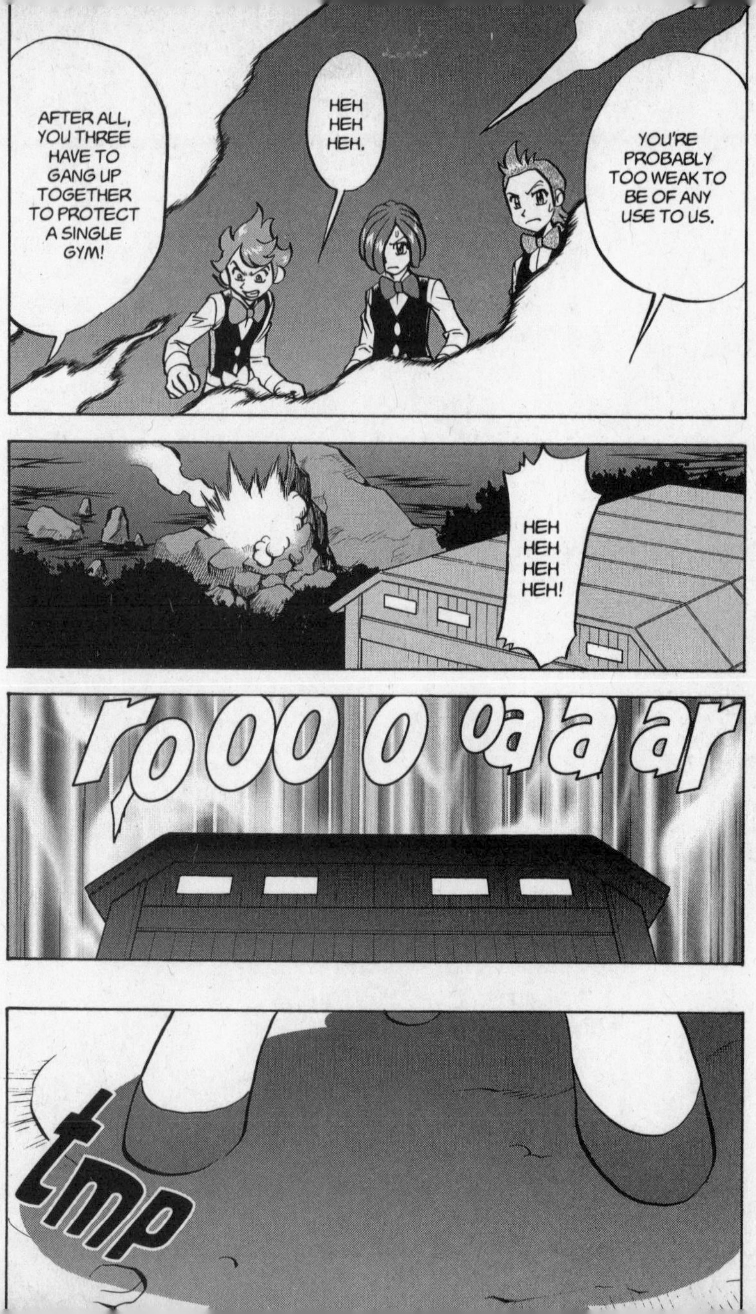
YOU'RE PROBABLY TOO WEAK TO BE OF ANY USE TO US.
HEH HEH HEH.
AFTER ALL, YOU THREE HAVE TO GANG UP TOGETHER TO PROTECT A SINGLE GYM!
HEH HEH HEH HEH!
ro oo o oa a ar
tmp

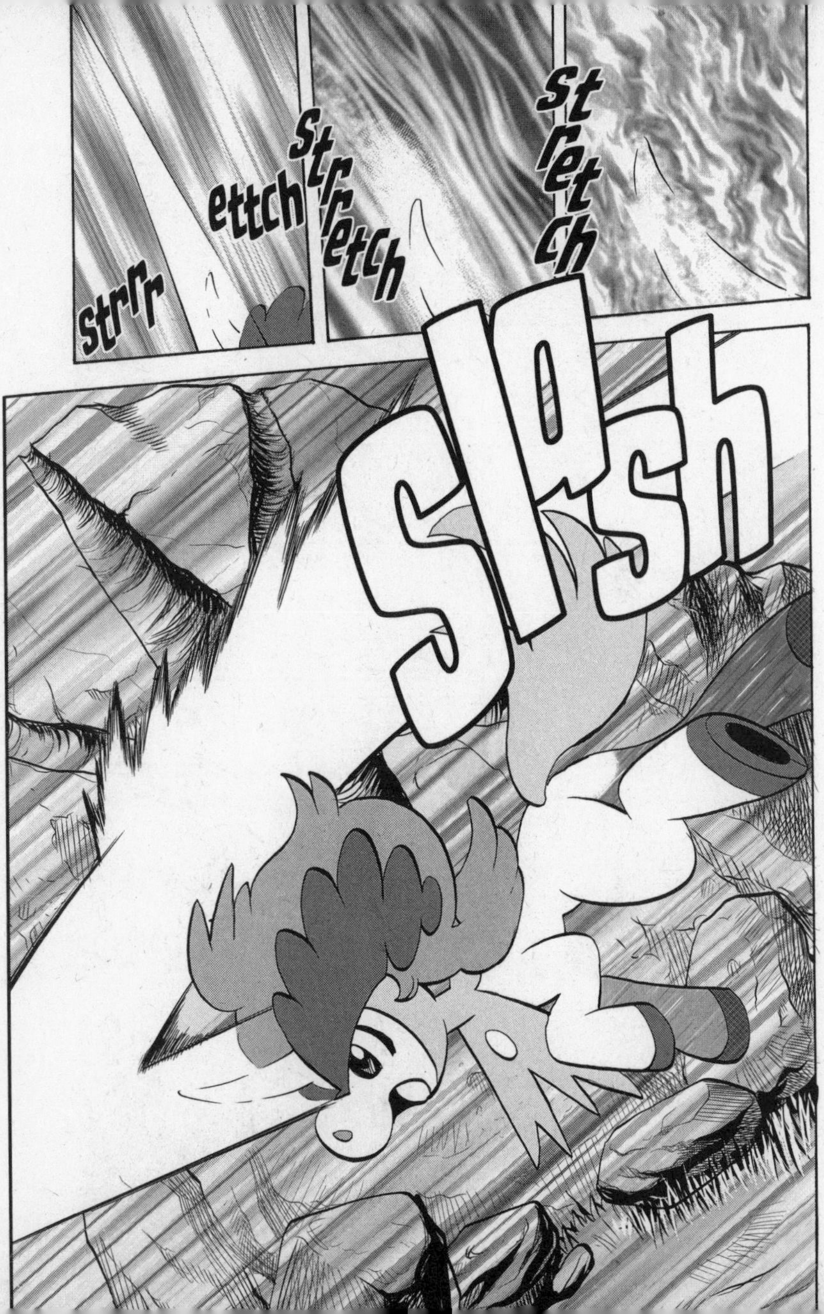
stretch
strretch
strrr
ettch
Slash

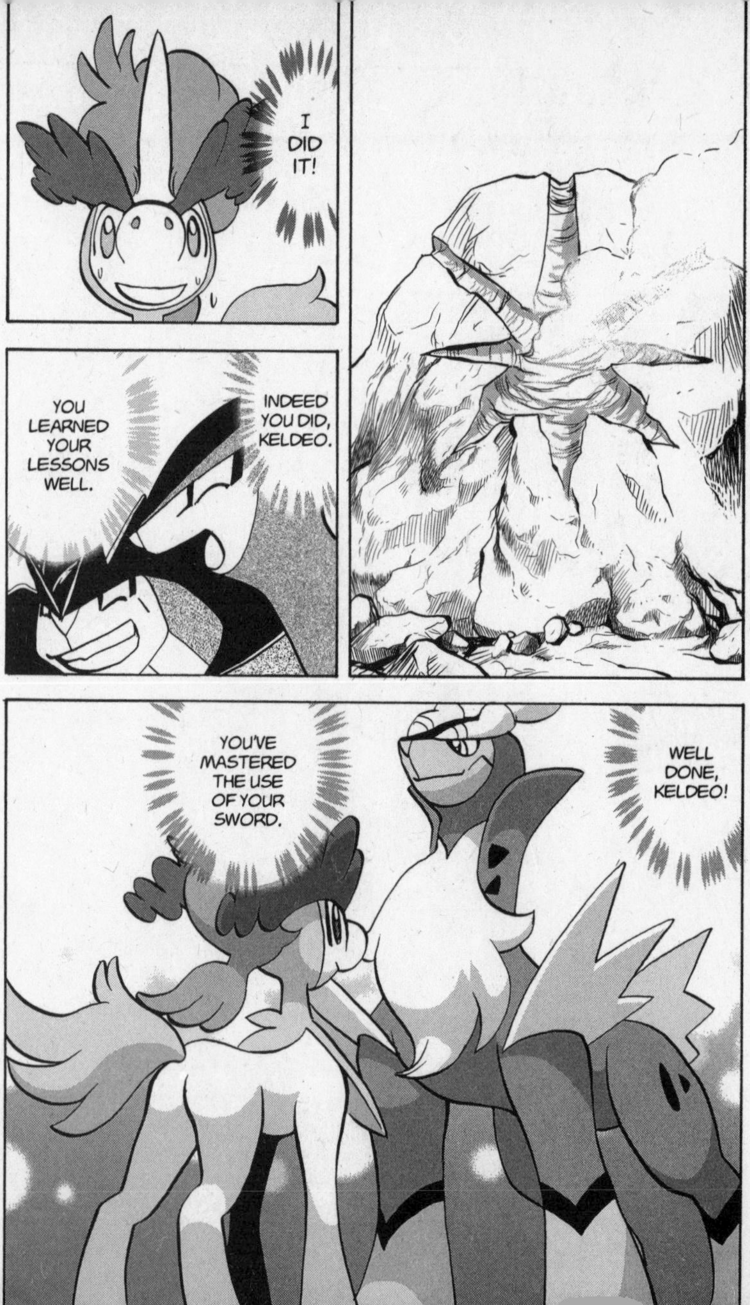
I DID IT!
INDEED YOU DID, KELDEO.
YOU LEARNED YOUR LESSONS WELL.
WELL DONE, KELDEO!
YOU'VE MASTERED THE USE OF YOUR SWORD.

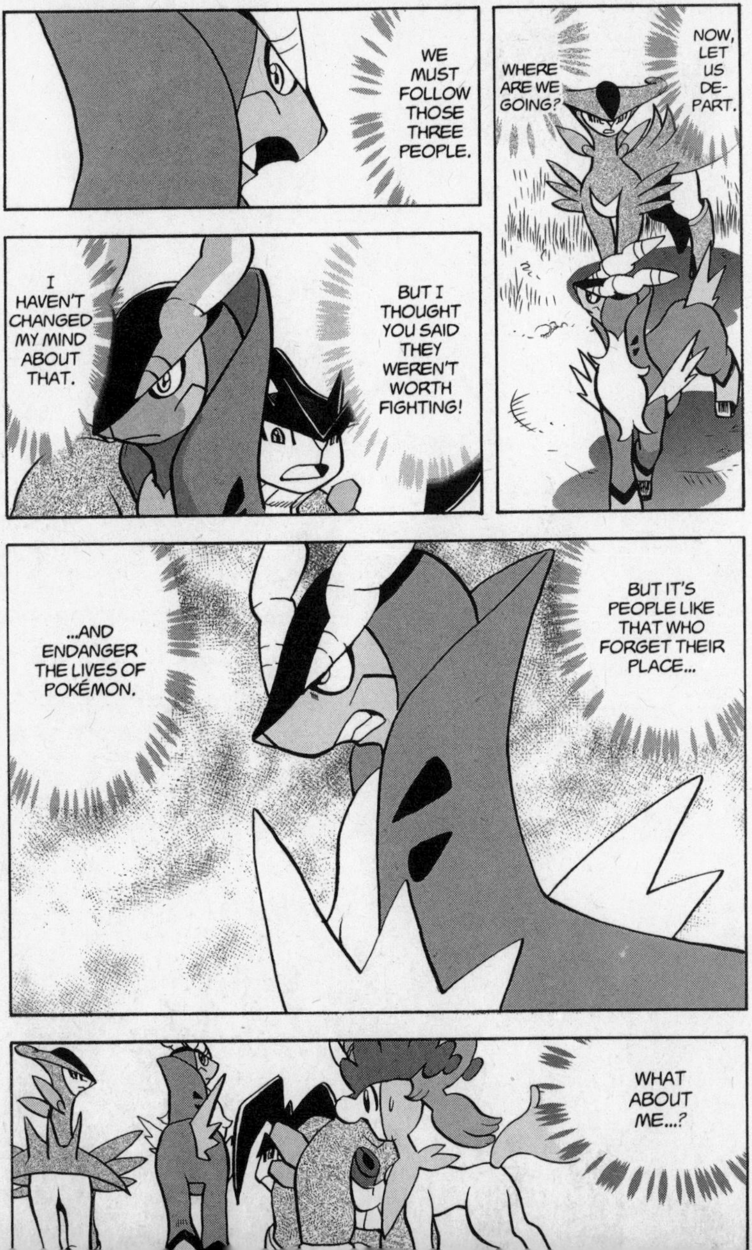
NOW, LET US DE-PART.
WHERE ARE WE GOING?
WE MUST FOLLOW THOSE THREE PEOPLE.
BUT I THOUGHT YOU SAID THEY WEREN'T WORTH FIGHTING!
I HAVEN'T CHANGED MY MIND ABOUT THAT.
BUT IT'S PEOPLE LIKE THAT WHO FORGET THEIR PLACE...
...AND ENDANGER THE LIVES OF POKÉMON.
WHAT ABOUT ME...?

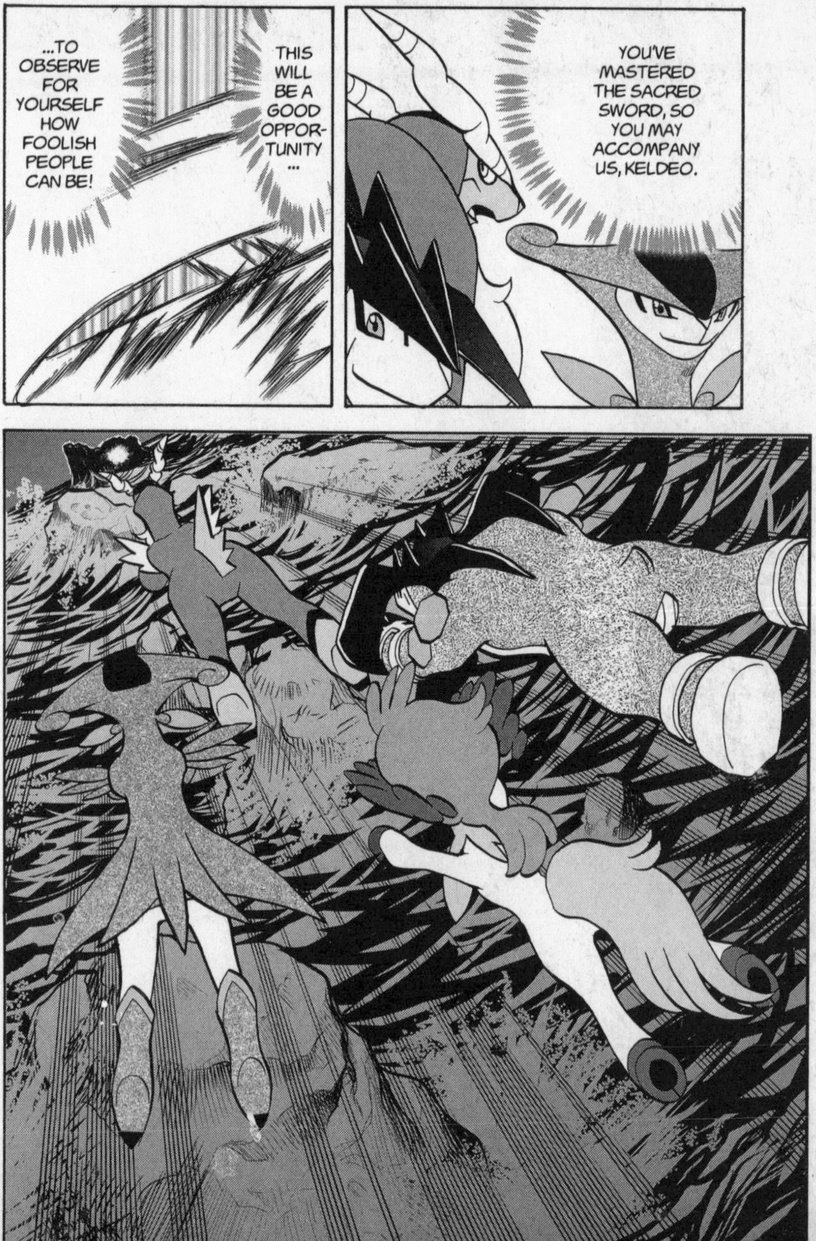
YOU'VE MASTERED THE SACRED SWORD, SO YOU MAY ACCOMPANY US, KELDEO.
THIS WILL BE A GOOD OPPORTUNITY...
...TO OBSERVE FOR YOURSELF HOW FOOLISH PEOPLE CAN BE!

dventures COMING SOON...

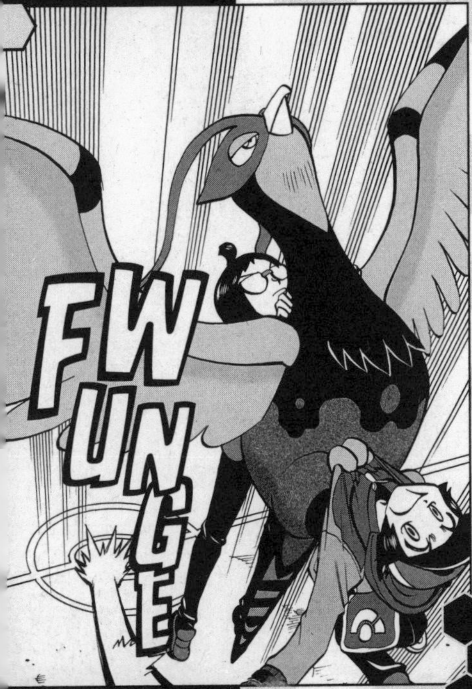

FWUNGE

non League battle,
ung friend Iris and
underestimated her
shocked to discover
eren is mistreating
his own Pokémon!
nis childhood friend

AND NOW, ONE OF BLACK'S FRIENDS IS *KIDNAPPED*!

Plus, watch the thrilling Pokémon League battles: Black vs. Iris and Hood Man vs. Cheren. Who will win and be pitted against each other?!

VAILABLE OCTOBER 2014!

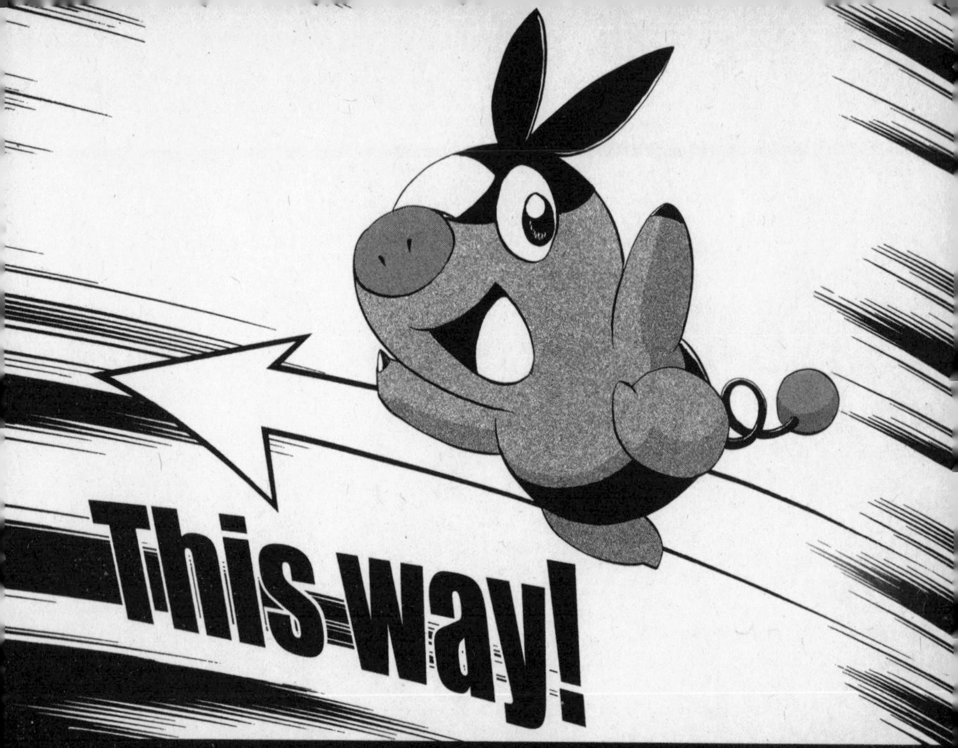
This way!

THIS IS THE END OF THIS GRAPHIC NOVEL!

To properly enjoy this VIZ Media graphic novel, please turn it around and begin reading from right to left.

This book has been printed in the original Japanese format in order to preserve the orientation of the original artwork. Have fun with it!

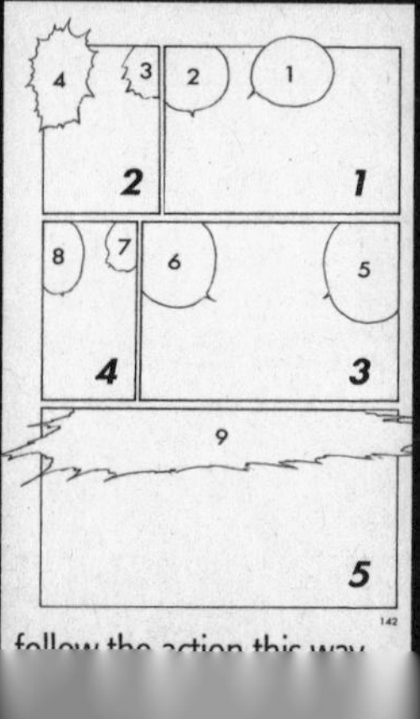